THE BLACK ATHLETE™

By John D. White

San Marcos California, 2016

Published by: Destined For Greatness Creative Writing & Publishing, LLC, San Marcos, California 2016

Published in the United States of America

The Black Athlete

Written by: John D. White

DEDICATION:

This book is dedicated to my Mother and Father, Gwendolyn and James White (deceased). Because of your example as parents, I know how to be an effective parent to my son Israel, and how to win at life. I will always love you both.

To my spiritual father and mentor Dr. Bishop Willie M. Thornton: Your example as a leader, father, and man of God has been the blueprint I have followed with reverence and respect. With that blueprint I've learned to succeed spiritually and naturally. I will be eternally grateful for your example and forever in your debt.

The Author at a glance

I (John D. White) began writing as a freshman in college. I used it as an outlet to express my thoughts, and allow my imagination to run free. I've always been a visionary, and one who always seen success in my mind, before the manifestation ever took place. I live by the saying, "You have to see it, before you see it, or you will NEVER see it." I believe that God has given me an innate ability to tell my story, by taking different facets of life to pen my first novel The Black Athlete.

Acknowledgements

*I would like to give honor to my Lord and Savior Jesus Christ for without Him none of this would be possible. I would also like to take this time to acknowledge some very important individuals. First, I would like to thank my family as a whole; my brother's (David, Timothy, Ricci, and Michael). My sisters; (Kimberly, Andrea, Jamilya, Crystal, Catherine, Chontelle, Sherry, Sharmatica, and Sheila). Additionally; my Aunts, Uncles, cousins, nieces, and nephews. The neighborhood I grew up in, on the Westside of Detroit, 7 Mile and Biltmore; you all helped raise me, and instilled grit and hard work in me, and I'm FOREVER grateful for you all! To Lindsey Hunter, Mike Mingrone, Eugene Brown, Willie Mitchell, Lamont Walker, Marvin Washington, James "J.C." Clark, Michael Mathis, lastly Marlon and Mario Woodard; you all are the brothers that helped me on this journey, that stood with me in the mist of adversity, and prayed me through times I thought I wasn't going to make it. I love you all to life! Additionally I would like to acknowledge my brothers of Pi Delta Gamma Fraternity Inc. To my enemies; I want to acknowledge you and say THANK YOU! There is no success without adversity, you helped me stay focused and pushed me to my destiny. Last, but not least. My heartbeat, my world, my reason to succeed in life, to my son **Israel Daniel Smith;** Son when you came into my world I was in AWE of you, I cried some nights as I watched you sleep, and I accepted the responsibility to be your Father. You motivate me to be a better person, a better son, a better coach, a better mentor, and one day a GREAT husband. You're my motivation son, and I love you with every fiber of my being.*

Finally I would like to acknowledge Louis Waters and Kenneth Ray; for their help in editing this work.

Warning—Disclaimer

Forward

Written from the heart of former NBA athlete, coach and 17 year veteran Lindsey Hunter. Hunter, who has known John D. White as a player, coach, community leader, and entrepreneur is now endorsing John D. White the author.

"The Black Athlete is the quintessential example of the mindset of the inner city youth. Coach White has embellished all the challenges and mindsets of our youth. John White is a great leader and has the ability to impact our youth. This book takes us on a realistic and imaginary journey into the minds and dreams of many of the kids in our country."

-Lindsey Hunter

"The Black Athlete although a fictional work has the ability to stretch the readers imagination and then bring you as the reader back to a place of reality. This work is one that examines the real life struggles and hardships that occur in the inner cities across this country. When reading this work it will take you through a plethora of emotion and forces the reader to look at aspects of life that aren't normally portrayed in other media outlets. It shows an aspect of the inner city that displays examples of positivity through both the African American family and the church however, it also reinforces the need for investment in the youth of the inner cities across this country. This work is to be commended and author John D. White should be proud of his ability to make this story come to life." "Kudos!"

-Author Denaryle Lovell Williams

Introduction

Like many African-American kids in inner cities, R.J. Watkins had aspirations of becoming a professional athlete. He saw it as his way out, his doorway to a better life, perhaps his only doorway. For R.J., it was more than just a dream, it was real. So real in fact, he could see it. He could feel it. He could taste it. Saying it out loud every now and then only reinforced it, validated it, and confirmed it to be true. "Someday, I'm going to play in the NBA!" R.J. declared. "I'm going to get my mom and dad out of this neighborhood, buy them a house, a car, and make sure they'll never have to work another day." Sammy, who had been R.J's best friend since he could remember, listened intently without saying a word. He had heard this declaration a hundred times as the pair walked home from school, maybe a thousand. Sammy had no rebuttal to such a bold prediction because as unlikely as R.J.'s declaration may have seemed, Sammy believed it, almost as much as R.J. did.

CHAPTER 1

As the sun went down, R.J. made one jump shot after another. He envisioned himself scoring baskets against NBA greats, and making game winning shots as the clock ran out. Growing up on the west side of Detroit, life was no cake walk, but the dream and desire to be a professional athlete drove R.J. each day. Nothing was going to stand in his way, not even the dark, which is why he strategically placed his basketball goal underneath the street light.

"R.J., do you see those street lights are on? It's time to come in the house!" his mother yelled. Kendall Simone Watkins, known as "Honey" by her friends and family, was born and raised in Grand Rapids, MI which was a three hour drive from the city. While laid off from her job as an insurance rep, Honey spent her days as a stay at home mother, taking classes to become a real-estate agent. Her parents had died when she was 4 years old in a car accident. So she moved to Detroit and was raised by her grandparent's, who instilled the calm and sweet demeanor inside of her that had a lasting effect on everyone she came in contact with. Her beautiful almond brown skin, long black hair, and breath taking beauty made her stand out in any crowd. She was always known as a quiet and soft spoken person, which made her that more attractive and fitted her name perfectly, "Honey."

Dripping with sweat, R.J. came inside. The Watkin's lived in a small two bedroom brownstone bungalow, in what was considered a middle to lower class neighborhood.

"Son, go in the bathroom and get cleaned up, dinner will be ready soon."

R.J. was the only child. Growing up he noticed how hard his father worked to provide for his family. During the down side of a recession, with the auto industry at an all-time low, jobs were very scarce in the city of Detroit. R.J.'s father worked twelve hour days driving a city bus, so a lot of responsibility fell on R.J. around the house.

Tap. Tap. Tap. Looking out of his bedroom window, R.J saw that it was Sammy. Samuel Burns had been R.J.'s best friend since they were toddlers. R.J.'s mother was Sammy's babysitter, which created a brother like bond between the two. Sammy knew that if he could depend on anybody, it was R.J.

"Sammy, what are you doing here?" R.J. asked.

"My mom and dad are fighting again, I had to get away," Sammy answered.

Sammy's mom and dad would often get into fights while drinking and partying, so he would either run to his room to bury his head under his pillow to escape the madness, or he would leave out the back door and flee down the street to R.J.'s house.

"If my Mom finds out you're here, I'll be in deep trouble," R.J. whispered.

"I just need to hang out for a little while, until things die down at home."

"Okay come on in, just keep it down, because if my Mom hears us, we both are dead! Check this out, I just got the new NBA 2K on Xbox, so we can play the game, but you have to keep it down Sammy," said R.J.

As they played the video game, R.J. and Sammy spoke about their futures, and how successful they would become. R.J. vowed to take Sammy with him when he made it to the NBA. This was something that drove Sammy crazy at times, because it had become like a broken record from hearing R.J. say it time and time again.

Sammy replied, "I might be the one taking you along."

They laughed.

"R.J., time to go to bed!" his mother shouted from the other room as they laughed.

With a look of panic R.J. said to Sammy, "Okay bro, you have to leave before my mom comes in."

As Sammy climbed out of the window, he looked back at R.J.

"Thanks for being here for me R.J., sometimes it feels like you are the only family I have."

R.J. smiled. "You are family bro, remember that. I'll see you later."

NEW BEGINNINGS...

The next morning, R.J.'s father, Ray, went into his bedroom to wake him.

"Get up son. There's work that needs to be done around the house." Ray Julius Watkins stood at a resounding 6 foot 4 inches tall, and his pleasant smile was what people called picture perfect. Ray was a strong yet sensitive man, who seemed to always know what to say at the right time, with the innate ability to defuse any situation. Born and raised on the west side of Detroit, his roots were southern. Ray's parents moved to the north from Birmingham, Alabama. Prior to his father becoming a minister, he worked in the auto industry as an engineer for Chrysler. Ray grew up not too far from where he and his family currently lived on Biltmore Street. He and Honey were long time sweethearts that met while they were freshman at Union High School, and they have been together ever since.

"Dad, it's too early in the morning to do work, can I please sleep in a little longer?" R.J. replied, with sleep in his eyes, and still tired from playing the video game late into the night.

"No son, we have a long day ahead of us, and remember, we have to go visit Kingdom Prep today, to see if you'll be attending High School there this fall."

With school almost two weeks away, R.J. wanted to sleep in as much as possible, but that didn't stop Ray from opening up the blinds to let some sunlight in.

"I also have to make a run to the grocery store," Ray continued. "So get up and get started on the yard, but not before you take a shower, because it smells terrible in here!"

When Ray arrived at the grocery store, he ran into an old friend from his work days at the Auto plant.

"Ray Watkins, is that you?"

"Hey Chuck, I haven't seen you in almost 5 years, how's life been treating you?" Ray said.

"All is well Ray, I'm still at the plant, and a lot has changed since you were there, and a lot has changed in my life as well. I got married, and I have twins now, a boy and a girl named Elijah and Elesha" Chuck replied. "Wow!" Ray said with excitement. "A lot has changed with you Chuck, I'm glad to know you're doing well."

Chuck could tell Ray was stressed out. He seemed tired and weary. Remembering how the church had hurt Ray, after his father lost his battle with cancer five years prior, Chuck was hesitant to invite him to church at Kingdom Ministries International (KMI).

KMI was one of the fastest growing ministries in the Metro Detroit area, and the Pastor was a world renowned speaker. Eventually, Chuck worked up the courage to extend Ray an invitation.

"Ray, I would like to invite you to my church, I believe you and your family would really enjoy it."

Ray took a deep breath.

"Chuck I don't know. I haven't been to church in years. I'm not even sure that God still knows me."

Although Chuck couldn't believe what he was hearing, he understood how Ray felt. "Don't say that Ray," he replied. "God will never leave you nor forsake you, my friend. Take some time, and think about coming out. In the meantime, I will text you the address." Ray nodded.

"Ok Chuck, I will think about it. By the way, it was good seeing you again." As Ray got into his car to drive home, thoughts of his father ran through his head, and the idea of visiting Kingdom Ministries weighed heavy on his mind. Ray said to himself that he'll mention it to Honey later, to see what she thought about it. Optimistic, Ray figured it probably wouldn't hurt to give it a try.

CHAPTER 2

It was already a hot day, yet the temperature continued to rise. Ray came home and saw that R.J. was in the yard working.

"Hey son, we have to get ready to go visit Kingdom Prep soon, so hurry up and finish the yard."

As R.J. finished up the yard, Sammy walked out on his porch and screamed down the street, "Hey R.J., I thought you were visiting that school today?"

While looking down the street in Sammy's direction, R.J. used his hand to block the sun from his eyes.

"I am. I'll be going in a little while. Lord knows I don't want to go! Why can't I just go to Union High like everyone else in the neighborhood?"

Although he asked the question, R.J. already knew the answer. His parents wanted him to have the best education possible, and Kingdom Prep was one of the premiere high schools in the country. It was even harder to get an interview to attend.

"Just go and have fun R.J., you might like it, you never know," Sammy said, as he tried to encourage him.

"Ok R.J., come on in and take a shower so we can get going, Mom has already laid your clothes out," said Ray as he approached the front door.

R.J. shook his head.

"Dad, do we have to go visit that school? What's wrong with going to Union High? You and mom went there…"

Ray looked into the eyes of R.J. who was visibly frustrated.

"Son, you don't understand our decision now, but one day you will appreciate your mother and I, for investing in your future."

Since Ray ran into his friend Chuck at the grocery store earlier that day, he questioned his own future. He hadn't been able to stop thinking about visiting Kingdom Ministries, even though Ray hadn't been to church since the passing of his father.

As they drove to Kingdom Prep for R.J.'s school visit, Ray said to Honey, "Babe, I'm thinking about us going to church on Sunday."

Happy, yet unsure of what to say, Honey looked to him with a confused but happy face. "That sounds great Ray. What made you come to that conclusion?" she asked. Ray sighed.

"I ran into Chuck at the grocery store," Ray explained. "He mentioned visiting his church, and I told him I would think about it. Since that conversation, it's been stuck in my head."

Honey knew that Ray struggled with going to church. Her prayer was that God would enter his heart, so that he would be open to attending church again someday.

"Well sweetie, I think it is a great idea that we go. So tell me, what church is it?" Honey asked.

"It's called Kingdom Ministries," Ray answered. "The Pastor there is young and has a powerful influence in the city. When Chuck mentioned that to me, it reminded me of what people always said about my dad, so I'm intrigued."

Ray's father was one of the most powerful preachers in the Detroit Metro Area during his time, and he was considered a landmark in the church. Once Chuck told him about KMI and Bishop Theo, he instantly thought about his father.

As they pulled up to Kingdom Prep, R.J.'s stomach turned due to anxiety. His dad looked back at him.

"We're here son. And don't worry, you'll be fine once you take the tour."

R.J. knew it would be a different environment, because until that point he had attended public schools his entire life, so he was unsure of what to expect.

"Dad, what if I don't like it, will I still have to go to school here?" R.J. asked, while still feeling nauseous.

"Well son that will be up to your mother and I to decide. Let's take the tour first, and we'll talk about that later," his father replied.

R.J. took a deep sigh. "Ok dad, I'm ready to go in."

Presently, the state's educational system was failing, and over 200 schools had closed down in the city of Detroit over the past several years. It was a challenge finding a good school. Kingdom Prep was an up and coming high school that excelled in academics, as well as in athletics. Those were the main reasons Ray and his wife wanted to send R.J. to school there. As the Watkins' entered Kingdom Prep, they instantly noticed the excellence and warmth of the school. As they walked down the hallway, they were greeted by the Head Master Mr. Whittier. With a noticeable smile on his face, Rudolph C. Whittier had a medium build and he wore black wired framed glasses, a brown suit, blue shirt, and a burgundy bow tie. He was one of the founders of Kingdom Prep Academy, and had been the Head Master since the schools existence. Even though he was short in stature, standing at an unintimidating 5 foot 8 inches tall, Mr. Whittier's voice was deep and powerful. If raised, it could shake the very core of a person.

"Hello, and welcome to Kingdom Prep," he said enthusiastically. "How can I be of assistance to you?"

Ray answered, "We're Mr. and Mrs. Ray Watkins, and this is our son R.J. We're here for a tour of the school that Coach Boyd set up for us. We were trying to locate the school gymnasium."

"Very well, if Coach Boyd set it up, I'm sure he'll be conducting the tour," Mr. Whittier said to Ray. Turning to R.J., "If your parents choose Kingdom Prep, you will love it here as a Student-Athlete, I'm quite sure of that," Mr. Whittier said confidently.

R.J. smiled.

"Well, I have to run, but it was a pleasure meeting you all. I look forward to seeing you again real soon," Mr. Whittier stated before walking off.

As R.J. and his parents continued down the hallway, R.J. knew they were getting closer to the gymnasium. He could hear the squeaking of gym shoes and the sound of whistles blowing. When they finally walked into the gymnasium, R.J.'s mind was made up. He looked around in amazement.

"Dad, this is where I belong," R.J. said while turning to his father. Ray laughed. "Son, we haven't even taken the tour yet." R.J.'s eagerness was apparent, so Ray said, "I have one question, and how do you know?"

With his mouth wide open, R.J. didn't reply, but the look in his eyes said it all. Kingdom Prep was his choice. Kingdom Prep was ranked #1 in the state in basketball and #6 nationally. The gymnasium was by far the best in the state, and it did something that no other school was able to do, it blew R.J. away.

CHAPTER 3

At 35 years old, Coach Thomas J. Boyd was regarded as one of the top coaches in the nation. Even though he was young, Coach Boyd knew how to connect with the boys he coached, as well as with the youth he came in contact with on a daily basis.

Kingdom Prep was an avenue for inner city kids to get a great education, and to be a part of an elite athletic program. Many of the students came from broken homes, others came from affluent families. At Kingdom Prep the two worlds were allowed to come together, which at times presented problems.

Coach Boyd blew his whistle to conclude practice. The young men ran to huddle around him. Dripping in sweat and exhausted from the two hour workout, the players listened attentively to what their coach had to say.

"Ok guys, way to compete and make each other better. As you see, we have a visitor here today. His name is R.J.

Watkins. Make sure you introduce yourself to him and his parents before you leave."

Kingdom Prep held their students to a very high standard academically and athletically. The opportunity that R.J. was getting was very hard to come by. Coach Boyd stumbled across R.J. playing basketball, while watching his nephew play in an A.A.U. basketball game.

"Mr. and Mrs. Watkins, it is a pleasure to see the two of you. R.J., how are you doing today?" asked Coach Boyd.

Coach Boyd stood at a resounding 6 feet 6 inches tall, as R.J. looked up to respond to him.

"I'm doing good Sir."

Sweating from being in the gym, Coach Boyd replied, "I apologize for the delay. If you can give me five minutes to clean up, we can get started with the tour."

Coach Boyd took the Watkins family on the tour. They were very impressed with Kingdom Prep's facilities and academic curriculum.

The tour concluded in the main office. "Bishop, how are you doing Sir," says Coach Boyd as they enter inside.

"I'm fine," he replies.

"Bishop, I would like to introduce you to Mr. and Mrs. Watkins, and their son R.J., we just finished their tour of the school."

"It's a pleasure meeting you, I'm Will Theo," the Bishop says as he extends his hand to Ray, and then to Honey.

Curious Ray asks, "As in Bishop Theo of Kingdom Ministries?"

Smiling, Bishop Theo says, "Yes, that would be me. Do I know you?"

Kingdom Prep was an extension of Kingdom Ministries. Ironically it was the church Ray was considering visiting on Sunday with his family. Ray knew that Bishop Theo was young, but at the age of 37, Bishop Theo was the Presiding Prelate of Kingdom Ministries International. There were more than 150 churches under him. Bishop Theo's spirit was that of a man two times his age. With just a hand shake Ray sensed the love and kindness that flowed from Bishop Theo.

Ray was seriously intrigued. "Bishop, my family and I would like to visit your ministry," he said. "And to answer your question, no I don't know you, but I've heard a lot of good things about you from my former co-worker Chuck Williams. I ran into Chuck earlier today at the grocery store and he invited me to visit the church. I just mentioned it to my wife on the way here."

"You and your family are more than welcomed to visit," Bishop said. "I look forward to seeing you all soon. Blessings."

As Ray drove home, he was amazed at how everything was coming together. Bishop Theo left a lasting impression on him and his family, and it was astonishing that Kingdom Prep was a part of Kingdom Ministries. Ray felt that R.J. would be safe and treated right at Kingdom Prep.

"Honey, I believe my mind is made up, as long as you're on board of course. I think that Kingdom Prep will be great for R.J. in a number of ways," said Ray.

Honey agreed, "I feel the same way, and R.J. obviously loved it during the tour of the school." It was evident that they both felt good about the decision.

Ray continued, "I will contact Coach Boyd and inform him of our decision, then we can take the next steps to get R.J. enrolled."

Sitting in the back seat, R.J. wore a big smile. Overcome with joy and excitement, he envisioned his future at Kingdom Prep.

CHAPTER 4

As the fall breeze began to pick up, R.J. stepped outside on his front porch. He looked down the street and saw Sammy working in the yard.

"Hey Sammy, what's up?" he yelled.

Sammy shakes his head, "R.J., it seems like these leaves will never stop falling. Look at your yard, it's spotless, but it seems like leaves just come up out of the ground down here."

As R.J. laughed, he went to his backyard and grabbed a rake, "Don't worry, I'll help you get the leaves up, and we'll be done in no time."

The wind seemed to get crisper and colder as the hours passed by. However, after about an hour, the leaves were all picked up. Sammy and R.J. finished raking up the last bit of debris, and then carried the bags filled with leaves to the curb.

"So tell me R.J., how did you like the school? Is it where you'll be going in a week?" Sammy asked.

R.J. nodded his head, "Yes, I'll be going to Kingdom Prep. I really liked the visit, and honestly I didn't think I would. There's something special about the place. Maybe it was the people, I don't know. I really liked the gym. You'll have to see it someday, its cold Sammy!"

It was a bitter-sweet moment for Sammy. Ever since the second grade, he and R.J. attended the same school. Now Sammy will be on his own in high school, which is a big leap for any teenager, especially without your best friend by your side.

"That's cool R.J. I'm glad you enjoyed yourself. It just really sucks that I won't have you around at Union High with me this year, or ever."

Saddened by Sammy's statement, R.J. felt guilty for thinking about only himself.

"Sammy, I will always be here for you bro, you will never have to worry about that. I'm just a few houses away. You're my brother and you will always be."

"I know R.J.," Sammy says, as they give each other a high five and a hug. "It's just going to be different without you around. Just know I'm happy for you, I really am bro. You better make sure you get me into your games for free! I know they charge an arm and a leg out there."

They both laugh.

R.J. replies "Don't worry Sammy. I will make sure you are there at every home game, I promise." Sammy looks around, "R.J. thanks for helping me with the yard. It would've taken me forever to finish without your help. Now I have to go in here and clean my room up before my dad gets home. I'll catch up with you tomorrow."

After making his way home, R.J. sat on the couch in the family room. Honey walked by. She noticed that he looked down.

"R.J., are you alright sweetie?" she asked. "You've been sitting in that same spot sulking for over an hour."

R.J. shrugged his shoulders.

"Mom, I'm ok, I guess. I was talking to Sammy today, and it's going to be different not having him around in school. With me going to Kingdom Prep, and him being at Union High, it's going to be a big adjustment for me even though I liked it there."

Listening to R.J., Honey looked at him and said, "R.J., that's life son, it's all about change and making adjustments. You going to Kingdom Prep shouldn't have an effect on your relationship with Sammy, especially if it's a true friendship. So hang in there son, everything will be just fine with you and Sammy, I'm sure of that."

Feeling encouraged, R.J. smiled from ear to ear.

"You're right Mom. I guess I felt bad for Sammy because I'm pretty much his only friend. I love you Mom, and thanks for the talk. Guess I'll get up now and shower."

Honey kisses him on the cheek. "I love you too son and a shower doesn't sound too bad, because you stink."

They laughed.

"Hey-hey-hey, I'm home." says Ray as he walked in the house.

Although Ray was exhausted from a long day of work, he was glad to be home with his family. Honey came out of the kitchen and greeted him with a kiss.

"Hey sweetie how was your day?" she said to Ray. "I made a plate for you and put it in the microwave."

"Thank you so much, you're the best…Lord knows I am starving right now." Ray was grateful to have such a wonderful wife. As he went into the kitchen to sit at the table, he asked where R.J. was.

While unwrapping Ray's plate, Honey explained to him the way R.J. was feeling about being away from Sammy for high school, and how difficult it is for him to be at a different school than his best friend.

Ray sat listening to her, then responded, "I can understand why he feels the way he does. They've been friends since we moved over here, but he'll be fine. We just have to keep him encouraged."

After Ray finished eating his dinner, he gave Honey a kiss on the forehead, then went and knocked on R.J.'s bedroom door.

"Come in," R.J. said.

Ray walked in, he said, "Hey son, how are you doing?"

Focused on his video game, R.J. replied, "I'm good dad, just playing this game, that's all."

Ray took a seat on the edge of the bed.

"Son, your mother told me about the talk you had with her concerning Sammy. The one about you being away from him for high school, and how awkward it's going to be at a school where you don't know anyone. All of that is normal R.J., but as your mother told you, it is a part of life and making adjustments. You and Sammy will be friends for a long time, so that shouldn't be a concern of yours."

R.J. put his video game on pause, and put his head down.

"Dad, I understand, I really do. It's just easier said than done. Just know that I'm going to be ok, and I'm looking forward to going to Kingdom Prep."

"Ok son," Ray said with a smile. "I just wanted to check on you, and make sure you were doing ok. Go ahead and get back to your game. Just make sure that you get some rest tonight. Love you son."

R.J. returned a smile.

"I love you too dad."

CHAPTER 5

Finally it's Sunday morning! The sound of gospel music filled the Watkins' home. This morning was different from other mornings, but it was refreshing. That type of atmosphere had been missing in the Watkins home for a long time.

It had been nearly five years since the Watkins family had attended church. The excitement and anticipation was great.

"R.J., wake up son, it's time to get ready," said Honey as she stuck her head in his room.

Dazed, confused, and still half asleep, R.J. tried to gather himself while wondering where the music was coming from.

Ray grew up listening to his parents playing gospel music on Sunday morning as the family got dressed for church. For him it was tradition, so it was only natural for him to do the same thing with his family.

Upon entering the family room, R.J. wiped sleep from his eyes and said, "Dad, what's with the music and why are you playing it so loud?"

Ray laughed.

"Son, this music is good for your soul. We all need a little more Jesus. Now go shower so we can get to church on time. I don't want to be late."

It wasn't long before Ray was dressed and ready to go.

"Alright, time to go R.J., and Honey I'm going out to start the car," said Ray as he grabbed his car keys off the kitchen table.

R.J. and his mother got into the car. It was evident how excited Ray was about going to church.

"Dad, I've never seen you this happy before, especially with that music this morning, it was SO loud!" said R.J.

Ray couldn't help but to laugh at what R.J. just said.

"Son, you just don't understand now, but in time you will. God has been good to us. Sometimes we feel like he's left us, but He's always there. I'm really looking forward to service today. I believe it will be great for our family and a fresh start for us."

As Ray pulled up to the church to find a place to park, he noticed how flooded the parking lot was. Scratching his head, Ray said, "It looks like we may not be able to find a seat once we get in."

At Kingdom Ministries, even if you were on time, you were still late. Every Sunday people came from all over the Detroit Metro area to attend church service and hear an inspiring message from Bishop Theo.

Eventually Ray found a place to park. Although it was a block away from the church, he was happy to have found one.

As they entered into the church, the Helps Committee greeted them saying, "Welcome to Kingdom Ministries, the place where God lives."

When Ray entered the sanctuary, he was amazed at how diverse the church was. There were people from many different nationalities. The purple carpet and seats, along with the gold crown modeling that lined the walls, gave KMI a look of royalty. As Bishop Theo walked in, he greeted everyone he walked by, and that intrigued Ray, because he noticed that Bishop Theo was touchable. At churches the size of Kingdom Ministries, rarely does a Pastor interact with the people.

Bishop Theo walked down the aisle. When he saw Ray and his family he said, "God bless you, I'm glad to see that you all came to visit today."

R.J.'s eyes were steadfast on Bishop Theo. He watched his every move, and he even noticed how his robe seemed to blow in the wind as he walked. The love at Kingdom Ministries was felt the moment they walked into the door. That was enough to convince Ray that this was where he and his family belonged.

After a wonderful service, Ray and his wife were inspired by Bishop Theo's message. Honey whispered to Ray, "Sweetie, I really enjoyed the service today."

Ray hadn't witnessed a church service like that in years, not since the days his father was pastoring almost 10 years ago.

"Yes, I really enjoyed the service as well. I'm looking forward to us coming back real soon," Ray replied.

As service was being dismissed, Ray spotted his friend Chuck in the sanctuary. They made eye contact, smiled and nodded their heads. As they walked towards each other, Bishop Theo walked down the middle aisle.

"Bless you Sir. Thank you for visiting today," Bishop Theo said to Ray.

Overjoyed, Ray extended his hand to Bishop Theo. "My wife and I really enjoyed the service today, and we will definitely be back."

Bishop humbly smiled. "I'm glad you and your family enjoyed the service. I look forward to seeing you again. Please excuse me. I have another assignment to get to."

Bishop Theo swiftly left the sanctuary. Ray and Chuck embraced each other.

"Ray, it's good to see you man," Chuck said. "I was talking to my wife about you this morning while we were getting ready for church." Ray smiled, then replied "Since that day I ran into you at the grocery store, visiting here has stayed on my mind." Chuck felt good about Ray coming to church. "Well Ray, it's great seeing you and your family here. I hope this isn't your last time." With a smile on his face, Ray says, "No, it won't be our last time Chuck, I promise."

CHAPTER 6

Still in amazement from the service, Ray said to Honey, "Babe that was an amazing service today, I haven't experienced church like that in a long time."

Looking at Ray with a smile on her face, Honey said, "Yes sweetie, it was a good service. So tell me, have we found a church home?"

With a convinced look on his face, Ray said, "I believe we have, and the youth church will be good for R.J. as well."

Ray glanced in the backseat through the rearview mirror at R.J., who smiled as he looked back at his dad through the mirror.

"Yeah Dad, I really like it there. The other kids were cool, and a lot of them go to Kingdom Prep."

Excited that everyone loved it at KMI, Ray said, "Well, Kingdom Ministries will be our new church home. We all loved it, and it'll be a fresh start for our family."

As Ray and his family pulled up to their home, R.J. noticed his friends playing basketball in the street. So that meant Sammy pulled R.J.'s basketball goal out of the backyard.

"Mom, Dad, can I change, then come back outside to play ball?" R.J. asked. "Sure son, that's fine with me, as long as your mother is ok with it," Ray said. "I don't mind R.J., go ahead and get out of those clothes, and I'll call you in when dinner is ready," said Honey.

Sammy saw R.J. getting out of the car and yelled down the street, "R.J., come play with us. You can be on my team. We need one more person to play."

Rushing in the house to change his clothes, R.J. said, "Give me a few minutes. I need to change my clothes, and I'll be right out."

As R.J. was changing his clothes, Honey stuck her head in his room, and told him to be careful while playing basketball outside. Many of the neighborhood kids were jealous of R.J., because of his basketball talents. They would often try to start fights with him on purpose.

"R.J., dinner will be ready in a few hours. That should be more than enough time to play ball," said Honey.

Even if he were alone R.J. would spend hours outside playing basketball. His passion to play basketball was genuine. Just as R.J. got ready to walk out the door, he stopped and looked at his mother.

"No need to worry Mom, I'll be fine while I'm out there playing, I promise."

As R.J. left out the house, Honey watched him from the window. Ray walked up behind her and said, "Window stalking again babe?"

Taking a deep sigh, Honey said, "Ray, I know R.J. is growing up, but I just don't like him playing basketball outside anymore. I know he needs to socialize and be with his friends, but the neighborhood isn't the same anymore. It's very dangerous now."

As Ray listened to Honey, he understood why she felt the way she did.

"Yeah, I understand sweetie, but he'll be fine. It's all a part of growing up, and a part of R.J. becoming a teenager. Don't worry," said Ray.

R.J. walked out to the street.

Sammy walked up to him and said, "Hey bro, why is your Mom looking out of the window?"

Shaking his head, R.J. said, "She doesn't like when I play street ball anymore, so she worries sometimes, that's all."

Acting as if he's big and bad, Sammy said, "You have nothing to worry about R.J., I'm out here with you. Besides, we've all been friends for years."

As R.J. dribbled the basketball, he told Sammy, "School starts tomorrow, and I'm not sure if I'm ready to go."

"Why not bro?" Sammy asked, wearing a look of amazement. R.J. answered, as he looked down while dribbling the ball. "I don't know, I'm just kind of nervous I guess. And on top of that, I don't know what to expect, especially with not really knowing anyone there."

Sammy released a sarcastic laugh, then offered words of encouragement, "Bro, you'll be fine. Look at it this way, at least you don't have to go to Union High, so count your blessings."

Taking a deep sigh, R.J. said, "Yeah, you're right Sammy, it's going to be fine."

"Yes it is bro, now let's play ball before you have to go in the house," Sammy replied, as he slapped the basketball out of R.J.s hands.

THE TROUBLEMAKER...

While they played basketball in the street, a group of guys came walking in their direction. The group stopped and stood on the curb to watch them play, they laughed and begun to trash talk, trying to irritate them.

The group was led by Jarrett, who was known in the neighborhood as J.J. He was a local troublemaker, who was always looking to start a fight. His older brothers were always in trouble and constantly in and out of jail.

"Hey Sammy! They shouldn't have picked you to play, your TERRIBLE!!" taunted J.J. as he tried to provoke him.

"Just ignore them bro, and let's keep playing," R.J. whispered to Sammy.

R.J. could feel the tension building, because Sammy had a temper, and things could go bad real quick.

Becoming irritated, Sammy said to R.J., "They just need to leave bro, J.J. is always causing problems, I'm about to shut him up if he don't chill out."

Looking at Sammy with a look of concern, R.J. said, "C'mon Sammy, not today. Let's just finish this game, and then we can go in the house."

Shaking his head, Sammy said, "Ok R.J., I hear you bro."

As the game ended, J.J. continued to talk trash to the guys. R.J. and Sammy ignored him as they took the basketball goal down. While they were pulling it to the back yard, R.J.'s mother yelled out the door for R.J. to come in for dinner.

"Aww, is Mommy calling the little baby in for supper?" taunted J.J. as his friends laughed.

By this time Sammy was getting upset, so he looked at J.J. and said, "Look man, why don't you chill out, you're always coming around here causing problems."

Getting in front of Sammy to redirect him, R.J. said, "Sammy, it's ok bro, let's just put this goal up, so we can go in the house."

As R.J. and Sammy continued pulling the basketball goal up the drive way, Ray came outside to see what was taking R.J. so long to come in.

He looked at them and could clearly see the frustration on their faces. Concerned, Ray asked, "What's going on guys? You seem to be bothered."

Without hesitation, Sammy turned and pointed his finger at J.J. and his friends, and said, "It's those guys Mr. Watkins, they're always coming around here causing problems, we can NEVER play in peace because of them!"

Ray looked over at J.J. and his friends, and said, "Ok guys, you all can go home now, the party is over."

Still standing on the curb, as if they didn't hear Ray, J.J. and his friends continued laughing and making jokes.

In disbelief at the disrespect shown, Ray steps off the porch and says forcefully, "Guys, I'm going to ask you one last time before I call the police. Please leave from in front of my home!"

Beyond irritated, Sammy dropped the basketball goal, and walked speedily towards J.J.

"Sammy!!" yelled R.J.

Focused on J.J., Sammy didn't break stride. He had clearly tuned out everything else around him.

"What is your issue man!?" Sammy yelled at the top of his lungs.

As Sammy got in striking distance of J.J. he cocked back his arm to deliver a punch. Ray raced over and grabbed Sammy from behind.

"No, no, no Sammy. Calm down! There's no need to fight him," said Ray. While trying to contain Sammy he looked over at J.J. and his friends. "Guys you need to leave and go home!"

J.J. and his friends laughed. After steadily trying to provoke Sammy, J.J. looked to his friends with a smug attitude and said, "Come on guys, let's get out of here before someone gets hurt."

While walking away, J.J. stopped and turned back towards Sammy. "I'll see you around Sammy. This ain't over. And next time Mr. Watkins won't be able to save you."

Shaking his head in disbelief, R.J. ran over to Sammy.

"Bro, you have to calm down. You know J.J. likes to start a fight, so he can have a reason to get somebody hurt. That's why he's always with a group of guys," said R.J.

Finally calming down, Sammy started to cry because he was embarrassed at the way he reacted to J.J. Sammy knows his temper can get the best of him, and it has gotten him in a lot of trouble in the past.

With his hand on Sammy's back, Ray told him, "It's ok Sammy. You just can't allow people to get you off your square like that."

Taking a deep breath, Sammy said, "I know Mr. Watkins. That guy just continues to bully us, and I just got fed up. I apologize for the way I reacted."

As they stood in the driveway, Honey stepped outside on the front porch. She noticed Sammy was crying and visibly upset.

"Ray, Is everything alright?" she asked.

"Babe, everything is ok now. Had a little altercation, but the boys are fine. I have to say, you were right about how unsafe it is in this neighborhood."

Exhaling deeply with a look of concern, Honey said, "Come on inside guys, dinner is ready. You're more than welcome to join us Sammy if you want to."

Still a little flustered, Sammy said, "No thank you Mrs. Watkins. I'm going to go home and lay down. I will see you all later."

As Sammy walked down the street and the Watkins went into their home, Ray looked at Honey and said, "You were right, it might be time to start looking for a new home."

CHAPTER 7

It's finally the first day of school. As Ray got up to get ready for work, he walked into R.J.'s room to wake him up.

"Son, it's time to get up. Today is your first day of school and you don't want to be late. Let's get a move on it."

Stretching and yawning, R.J. got up and headed to the bathroom.

"Dad, I don't know whether to be nervous or excited. Everything is going to be so new, especially wearing a uniform."

At Kingdom Prep, all of the males were required to wear a blue blazer, khaki pants, a white shirt, with a red, yellow, and blue striped tie. Most of the students weren't fans of the uniform policy there.

"Son, look at it this way, it's preparing you for the real world. One day you're going to have a job, and you might be required to wear a shirt and tie," said Ray.

R.J. shook his head at his father's comment.

"Well, I have a while for that Dad, so until then, I don't want to wear it."

While laughing at R.J., Ray replied, "Such is life son. Now get in the bathroom and get cleaned up. And that means taking a shower and brushing your teeth!"

While R.J. was finishing up in the bathroom, Ray got dressed, and Honey was in the kitchen preparing breakfast.

As Ray walked in the kitchen, he kissed Honey on the cheek.

"Good morning babe. It sure smells good in here," Ray said, as he reached for a piece of bacon.

Honey slapped his hand away.

"No-no-no Ray. No touching the food. Breakfast will be ready soon."

Laughing at her, Ray went back to his bedroom to finish getting dressed for work.

Finally getting out of the shower, R.J. smelled the food that his Mom was cooking. He hurried to his room so he could get dressed and eat breakfast. Once in his room R.J. heard a knock on his bedroom window. He looked to see who or what it was. To his surprise, it was Sammy.

"Sammy, what are you doing out there at this time of the morning?" R.J. asked, wearing a look of confusion.

R.J. could tell that something was wrong with Sammy; he didn't look like himself. Something was definitely troubling him.

"You know us Public School kids have to catch the city bus, so we have to be up extra early," said Sammy.

"Yea, I guess you're right Sammy, but why are you outside of my window, and not at the bus stop?"

With a look of concern on his face, R.J. stared at Sammy steadily awaiting his reply.

Looking down at the ground and taking a deep breath, Sammy said, "I'm afraid to go to school. J.J. and his crew keep threatening me, and I don't know what's going to happen."

Wishing there was something he could do, R.J. stood there speechless. Afraid for Sammy, all he could do was look at him.

"I don't even know if I'm going to school today R.J., I might just skip once my parents leave for work," said Sammy.

R.J. shook his head, as he listened to Sammy talk.

"Sammy, please go to school. Don't let that guy bully you, and cause you to miss school, especially if you want to play basketball."

Sammy's mind was pretty much made up about not going to school. Many young children had to fight going to school, and they had to fight coming home. To many, that was a way of life on the west side of Detroit. You had to persevere or get swallowed up by the streets. For R.J. Watkins, going to

Kingdom Prep was a blessing and escape from the everyday routines of the hood.

After Sammy left, Honey called R.J. to the kitchen so he could eat breakfast. Sitting at the kitchen table, Ray looked at R.J. with excitement about his fresh start at Kingdom Prep.

"Hey son, are you ready for your big day at school?" Ray asked. "I know you're excited, because I am."

Bobbing his head in agreement with his father, R.J. said, "Yeah Dad, I am a little excited. I'm also nervous, because it'll be my first day at a new school."

Adjusting to Kingdom Prep would be challenging for R.J., but his father always instilled in him to adapt to change, because that's what life was all about.

Ray looked at R.J. and said, "Son, you'll be fine. Just look at it as a new beginning. Enjoy it. A lot of kids wish they could be in your position."

As they finished up their breakfast, Ray told R.J. to grab his book bag so they can get ready to go. R.J. ran to his room to grab his bag while his mother was bagging his lunch.

R.J. went towards the front door to leave.

"Son, aren't you forgetting something?" Honey said.

Looking back at his Mother, R.J. said, "Oh. I'm sorry Mom," and he kissed her on the cheek.

Noticing that she had a bagged lunch in her hand for him, R.J. said, "Mom, I'm in high school now, I can't take a bagged lunch to school. Besides, I get free lunch, so I'll just eat with everyone else."

Smiling and admiring the fact that R.J. was growing up, Honey said, "Okay son, enjoy your day at school, and I'll be there to pick you up at 3 o'clock, love you."

"I LOVE YOU TOO!" R.J. yelled back as he ran out the door.

As Ray backed out of the drive way, he noticed Sammy sitting on his front porch. "Why isn't Sammy in school?" he thought to himself.

Ray rolled down his car window and said, "Hey Sammy, what time do you supposed to be at school? You need a ride?"

As R.J. sat in the passenger seat, he already knew what Sammy's plans were, and what he had told him earlier that morning.

Looking down at the ground as he threw rocks, Sammy said, "No Sir, I don't need a ride, but thank you."

Feeling like something wasn't right with Sammy, Ray with a look of concern said, "Ok… make sure you make it to school, because it's the first day, and you don't want to miss it."

Waving at Ray and R.J., Sammy said, "Ok Mr. Watkins, I'll see you all later."

Sammy stood in the walkway in front of his home, trying to figure out an acceptable excuse to give his parents once they find out he didn't go to school. The school always called the parents when a student didn't show up to school.

Pacing back and forth, he rehearsed one excuse after another. "Mom and Dad, I lost my I.D. card. I knew they wouldn't let me in school, so I just came back home." He shook his head. That's not going to work. Sammy became frustrated and anxiety started to kick in. "Maybe I should just go to school," Sammy thought to himself. With over 1200 students at Union High, Sammy figured it's a great chance he won't even see J.J. at school. After thinking about it long and hard, Sammy finally decided to go to school.

CHAPTER 8

As R.J. walked through the hallway to get to class, he was approached by a few of the basketball players; however, the introduction wasn't as polite as R.J. thought it would be.

Jason Moses, whom everyone called J-Mo, was the star basketball player at Kingdom Prep. He didn't take it too well, when he heard about this star freshman named R.J. Watkins. With broad shoulders, supreme athleticism, and standing at 6 feet 4 inches tall, J-Mo was a senior from Southfield, a suburb that was separated from Detroit by 8 Mile road. Even though it was close, it seemed to be so far away because of the drastic difference in the neighborhoods. J-Mo's parents were engineers at Chrysler, so money was no issue in his household. He and R.J. came from two different worlds, and they were on a collision course to gain supremacy as the man on Kingdom Prep's basketball team.

"So, you're the new kid everyone's talking about?" said J-Mo.

As R.J. looked at him, he extended his hand. "What's up, I'm R.J."

J-Mo stared at him with a grim look and a chuckle, and then uttered, "That's nice, but you need to know that this is my school and my team. Besides, I don't shake freshmen's hands."

Unfazed, R.J. walked away shaking his head. He found some joy in knowing that a senior was intimidated by him. Eventually R.J. made it to class. He took a seat towards the front, and then reflected on what his father told him on the way to school.

"Don't sit in the back of the class, because that will send the wrong message to the teacher, because you're an athlete."

"Hey, what's up man?" A voice interrupted R.J.'s moment of reminiscing.

He glanced to his right to see a tall skinny white kid named Reginald Curtis, but everyone called him Reggie.

While extending his hand, R.J. said, "What's up bro, my name is R.J., and you do shake freshmen's hands right?"

Reggie was one of the guys with J-Mo in the hallway, when he approached R.J. moments earlier.

Reggie smiled. "Of course I do man. My name is Reggie and I'm a sophomore. Don't pay J-Mo any attention. He did the same thing to me last year. I guess it's a form of freshmen hazing."

"Well he needs to chill on me. I'm here to go to school and play basketball, not to worry about an insecure dude."

Reggie laughed. "I tell you this much R.J., you handled it better than anyone has, and I think you bothered him more by looking at him and walking away."

R.J. looked back at Reggie with a blank stare.

"Well he better get used to it, because I'm not wasting my energy."

As the bell rang, everyone headed to the Auditorium for an assembly to welcome everyone back to Kingdom Prep for the new school year. This year's speaker was Bishop Theo. As R.J. walked into the auditorium, he noticed that a lot of the students were members at Kingdom Ministries. When Bishop Theo walked on stage, R.J.'s eyes lit up, because he was so intrigued by him.

The students sat and listened attentively as Bishop Theo spoke. He ended his speech by saying, "You are a master piece, because you are a piece of the Master." With that came a standing ovation from the student body, and everyone left the auditorium inspired and ready to have a great school year.

As R.J. and Reggie walked to class from the assembly, R.J. asked, "Hey, do you go to Kingdom Ministries?"

"Nah," Reggie answered, focusing on the ground, as if he was daydreaming. "We go to this boring church out by the mall in Troy. The services are held in the local recreation center out there."

R.J. could tell that Reggie wasn't too excited about his church, so R.J. said, "Well, maybe you're Mom and Dad will let you visit one day. My parents LOVE it there bro, and I mean they LOVE it."

They laugh.

Reggie answered, "Yea bro, I'm hoping they get tired of it one day."

As they split to go in opposite directions, Reggie turned back around and said, "R.J., don't forget we have open gym today after school. Make sure you're there on time."

R.J. nods his head, "I got you bro. I actually forgot, but I'll call my Mother to let her know. I'll see you there."

MEANWHILE AT UNION HIGH...

It was second hour when Sammy finally made it to school. As he walked into the building, the hallways were crowded as if there were too many people occupying the space. After passing through the metal detectors, which were the norm in the Detroit Public Schools, he was approached by a security guard. The guard informed Sammy that he had to report to the office because of his tardiness. With each step that Sammy took toward the office, he felt as if he were in a foreign land. He didn't recognize anyone in the school, even though it was over a thousand students at Union High.

Once Sammy was checked in at the office, he was given his schedule and had his I.D. picture taken. While walking to class, Sammy came across the one person he had hoped to avoid.

J.J. was standing up against the locker. When he saw Sammy, surprisingly he didn't say anything. Sammy was so thrown off by J.J.'s reaction, or lack thereof, Sammy, turned back around to see if that was really J.J. standing there. Confused but relieved, Sammy went in class and took his seat. In the back of his mind he knew something wasn't right with J.J.

As class went on, Sammy thought about R.J., and how things were going for him at Kingdom Prep, but his mind kept going back to J.J. He couldn't figure out why he was acting so strange in the hallway. Sammy knew that J.J. couldn't be trusted, so he planned to play it safe and try to avoid him at all cost.

When the bell sounded, it was time for lunch. While walking out of the classroom, Sammy ran into one of his friends from middle school.

"Hey Isaiah, I didn't know you came to Union," said Sammy.

With a look of disappointment on his face, Isaiah looked at Sammy and said, "Yea man, this is not where I wanted to be, but my dad couldn't afford a private school. Even though he knows it's dangerous, there was nowhere else for me to go."

Sammy replied, "Yea, R.J. actually wanted to come to school here at Union, but his Mom and Dad told him no, so he's at that school out in the suburbs called Kingdom Prep."

With a look of amazement on his face, Isaiah said, "Kingdom Prep, as in "the" Kingdom Prep? His parents must bring in some serious bank."

Laughing at Isaiah, Sammy looked at him and said, "Not at all bro. He's a really good basketball player, so he received a scholarship to play ball there. His parents took advantage of the opportunity. To be honest, I can't blame them, because it sucks here."

Isaiah shook his head in agreement. "Yea bro, it really does suck here. I wish I had played a sport," he says laughing. "...then I wouldn't have to attend this terrible school."

It was lunch time, and the smell of cheeseburgers and tator tots filled the air. As Sammy and Isaiah walked into the lunch room, Sammy spotted J.J. sitting at a table with some of his friends. This time J.J. looked at Sammy with a grim look, and stared at him all the way across the lunch room.

Taking notice of the look that J.J. gave Sammy, Isaiah said, "Hey bro, I think somebody in here doesn't like you…"

Taking a deep sigh, Sammy said, "Yea man, I know he don't like me, but it's cool... That guy is always trying to cause problems, and it started in the hood."

Walking right beside Sammy, Isaiah said, "Well bro, if anything goes down, I have your back, so don't worry about nothing." Short and stocky, Isaiah was rough around the edges, and the type that never backed down from a fight. It was known that his brothers were members of 7 Mile Dogs, a local gang in the city of Detroit, so Sammy was in good company if he needed back up.

Nodding his head at Isaiah, Sammy said, "I appreciate that bro, but I'm not worried about him. I just don't have the time or the energy to be fighting every day." Isaiah looked at Sammy with a perplexed facial expression. "What do you mean fighting him every day?"

With a stoic look on his face, Sammy said, "When dealing with a guy like J.J., you don't fight him just one time. You will have to fight him every time you see him bro."

BACK AT KINGDOM PREP...

Meanwhile at Kingdom Prep, as school was letting out, R.J. was looking forward to going to open gym, and having the opportunity to play against the guys for the first time. As R.J. walked into the locker room for the first time, he saw his locker with his name posted over it. He was pumped.

Kingdom Prep had one of the largest Nike contracts in the nation amongst high school programs, so everything was top of the line for the student-athletes. As the boys went out on the court to warm up, J-Mo came into the gym and said, "No freshman can be on my team, PERIOD."

As R.J. jogged back up the court, he looked at J-Mo and said, "That's fine with us, we should play upper classmen vs. lower classmen, that way it'll be even."

"Look freshman," J-Mo said, while laughing at R.J.'s suggestion. "...you don't have a say so about what we do here. Are you even on the team yet?"

R.J. put his head down and took a deep breath and said, "We'll find out soon if I'm on the team or not. And you'll see after we play today who's the best player in Kingdom Prep."

DEAD silence overtook the gym. The boys couldn't believe R.J. spoke to J-Mo in such a disrespectful way. Everyone knew that it was going to be a problem. Most of the guys were intimidated by J-Mo, because he was All-State and a McDonald's All-American candidate. However, none of that phased R.J., because he felt he was just as good when it came to playing basketball. R.J. was always taught to be a legend in his own mind, and to see the success before he ever experienced it.

The confidence that was inside of R.J. bothered J-Mo, but he couldn't help to notice how R.J. reminded him of how he used to be, when he first came to Kingdom Prep.

As they played, R.J. and J-Mo went at each other like they were enemies on the street, instead of teammates on the top high school team in the state. However, they both left the gym with a mutual respect for each other's game, but it was only the beginning of their on the court battles.

CHAPTER 9

It was a cold crisp fall weekend, and R.J. stepped out on his front porch to take in some fresh air. Ever since going to Kingdom Prep, R.J. made some new friends, and his basketball teammates had become his second family. Rarely did R.J. see Sammy, even though they lived two houses down from each other. So R.J. decided to go down to Sammy's to see if he was there. R.J. knocked on the door, but no one answered. He walked around to Sammy's bedroom window and when R.J. looked inside, he noticed Sammy was lying on the bed. When he looked closer, he couldn't believe what he saw Sammy doing. R.J. knocked on the window, and Sammy jumped up startled. He unlocked the window to open it, and smoke rushed out of the window followed by the smell of marijuana.

R.J. looked at Sammy in disbelief then asked, "Sammy, when did you start smoking weed bro? What's going on with you?"

Obviously high, Sammy looked at R.J. and said, "I don't know man. It's been a while now. I just do it to get through my day bro."

Still in amazement, R.J. just looked at Sammy unsure of what to say next.

Offended by the blank stare and silence, Sammy says, "Look R.J., don't come over here judging me bro. It's only weed. It's no big deal. Besides, when was the last time I seen you, "Best friend?"

"What's that supposed to mean? You're blaming me for you smoking weed? R.J. asked, completely caught off guard by the question. "Look Sammy, I wasn't judging you, and as for me not seeing you, I'm at school or practicing all the time bro. It's nothing personal. I'm just BUSY, literally all the time Sammy! School, church, basketball, and everything else comes with living my life!"

A sarcastic laugh escapes Sammy. "Well, I guess that's what happens when you become a superstar huh?"

R.J. just shook his head and walked away leaving Sammy looking out of his bedroom window. As R.J. made his way back down the street, Sammy came out on his front porch and yelled, "I thought you'd always be there bro, but I see you're too big time for us little people now!"

Turning around, R.J. looked back at Sammy in disgust. "Get it together Sammy. That weed is messing with your head. Just get it together bro!"

Later that evening R.J. sat in the family room. Ray walked in and noticed R.J. looking disturbed.

"Hey son, it looks like something is on your mind. What's going on?"

Lying back on the couch, with his hands on his head, and his eyes closed, R.J. said, "Dad, it's a lot of things going on. First, I'm dealing with this clown on the basketball team named J-Mo, who thinks he can run the team by intimidating everybody. Then I go down to Sammy's house because I haven't seen him in a while, only to find him smoking weed in his bedroom. He then blames me for his weed addiction, and accuses me of judging him. On top of that, he had the nerve to say, he smokes weed because he hasn't seen his "best-friend" in a long time. So tell me, HOW CRAZY IS THAT?"

Taking a seat on the couch next to R.J.'s out stretched legs, Ray looked at R.J. "Son, it sounds like you're growing up."

R.J. looks to his father confused. "Dad, how is that growing up?"

Smiling Ray answers, "The older you get, the more adversity you will face in life. People will irritate you. They'll dislike you for no reason. Friends that were close to you, at some point fade away, but you'll make new ones. That's just life son, and a part of growing up."

Listening to what his father had said, R.J. still couldn't get over the fact that Sammy did him like that. Looking up at the ceiling, R.J. said to his father, "Dad, Sammy was acting like a totally different person; he doesn't even look the same. I'm really worried about him."

After a deep sigh, Ray responds, "Son, all you can do is pray for him. Sammy is battling a lot of demons, and that's a lot to deal with, especially at his age."

While sitting on the sofa pondering what his father had said about Sammy, R.J. couldn't help but to feel sorry for his friend. A sense of guilt came over R.J., because he felt like he wasn't there for him.

As if he could read R.J.'s thoughts, Ray said to him, "Son, it's not your fault that Sammy is the way he is. He made the choice to do those things, and he has to make the choice to stop."

Looking up at his Dad, R.J. said, "I know Dad. I just feel bad for him. I really do."

The weekend came, and Sunday service at Kingdom Ministries was great as usual. Ray sat back and started pondering on the way things were shaping up for him and his family. Work was going great for him. He had received a promotion to Terminal Manager from being a City driver, which meant he received a huge pay raise. Honey was close to completing her certification to become a Real Estate agent, and R.J. was in one of the best high schools in the country, while excelling on the basketball court. It seemed as though life was perfect, and everything was FINALLY falling into place for his family.

As Ray and R.J. sat at the kitchen table, Ray couldn't contain his excitement about R.J.'s first high school game, which was coming up in two days. "So are you excited about the game on Tuesday?"

With a huge smile on his face, R.J. looked at his Father and said, "Dad, you have NO idea how excited I am. I know I'm not going to be able to sleep tomorrow night. I'll be up thinking about the game all night."

"That's normal son," Ray said laughing. "Just be sure to embrace the moment, because it's your first high school basketball game. You'll be starting as a freshman. Know that we're very proud of you son."

R.J. nodded his head, and said, "Thanks Dad."

As the night came to an end, Ray sat up in the bed talking with Honey. They spoke about how everything was coming together for them, and how God has blessed them in such a short period of time. It seemed like just yesterday when Ray ran into Chuck at the grocery store, and he invited him to Kingdom Ministries. Ever since that day, things have begun to change for the better in Ray's life.

Excited about everything and happy that Ray isn't stressing anymore, Honey said to him, "Well sweetie, tomorrow will be your first day as Terminal Manager. I know you're excited, and I am confident that you will be awesome!"

Ray smiled as Honey rubbed the top of his head, and then replied, "You know babe it really hasn't sunk in yet. And I really don't know what to expect. I just don't know how guys will react to me being in that new position. There may be some jealousy. You know how people can be."

Honey grabbed him by the hand and looked deep into his eyes. "Ray, you were made for this. God has you right where He wants you to be. Don't worry about other people, and what they are thinking or saying. You're not there to please them, but to do a job."

With a huge smile on his face, Ray grabbed Honey affectionately and said, "Baby, that's why I love you, you make me feel like I can conquer the world. I love you."

While kissing Ray, Honey whispered softly to him, "I love you too."

CHAPTER 10

It was finally game day at Kingdom Prep. The opponent would be inter-state rival and powerhouse Detroit City Institute. The day started with a Pep Rally in the field house and the atmosphere was unbelievable. It took R.J.'s breath away. The support that Kingdom Prep received from the community, as well as from the alumni was like none other. The band was second to none as they played loud and passionately. The cheers and pure excitement that filled the air made for a night to remember at Kingdom Prep.

As Coach Boyd came to the microphone, he attempted to settle the crowd down because the cheers were SO loud. He then addressed the crowd, thanking them for their continual support throughout the years. Coach Boyd went on to introduce the Kingdom Prep High school boys' basketball team. The roars and the cheers echoed throughout the whole school as he called the names of the players. When he got to R.J., the Fieldhouse erupted!

R.J. had become so popular because he was the only freshman on varsity, and not only that, he was the starting point guard for the #6 team in the country. With all of the attention and recognition, came a lot of jealousy and envy towards R.J. It started with his teammate J-Mo, and pretty much ended on his own block, with his old friend Sammy. All R.J. wanted out of life was to make it to the NBA, so his parents didn't have to work another day in their life. However, he learned quickly, that to whom much is given, much is required of them.

As R.J. and some of the basketball team walked to class from the Pep Rally, R.J.'s friend Reggie said, "Bro, did you hear how they screamed and cheered for you when Coach called your name? Dude, the look on J-Mo's face was priceless."

Shaking his head R.J. replied, "I could care less bro, just like my Dad always told me, people will love you today, and hate you tomorrow, so it's a must that you always stay humble Reg. Right before the Pep Rally, Coach Boyd pulled me and J-Mo in his office and we squared things away. He told us to get it together, because a kingdom can only be destroyed from the inside out. So there shouldn't be any more issues with us."

Reggie listened to what R.J. said to him, like he always did many times before. Even though Reggie was a year ahead of R.J., he looked up to him, and valued the things R.J. said. R.J. was a product of the inner city, while Reggie was a product of the suburbs. Their worlds came to a common ground at Kingdom Prep, because regardless of your upbringing, or your parent's financial status, at Kingdom Prep everybody was on the same level and at the same place.

GAME TIME...

"Come on Honey, we can't be late to R.J.'s first game, the place will be jammed pack," yelled Ray from the kitchen as he grabbed a soda from the fridge. If anyone was excited about R.J.'s game, it was Ray. He had told ALL of his coworker's about the success R.J. was having at Kingdom Prep, and how great the team was going to be this year. He knew how important this game was to R.J., and the opportunity he was given to play at Kingdom Prep. R.J. looked forward to this moment since the beginning of the season. The hard work he put in during the preseason showed how determined he was to be successful at Kingdom Prep.

Racing out of the room, while putting her jacket on, Honey said, "Ok Ray, I'm ready to go." Wearing a shirt that read "Kingdom Prep Mom", Honey was just as excited about the season as Ray was.

While walking out to the car, Ray and Honey noticed a crowd of people standing down the street accompanied by three to four police cars that were parked on the street.

As they looked to see what the commotion was all about, their neighbor, Pops, yelled out from across the street, "These kids are out of control Ray, this neighborhood isn't what it used to be, every time you turn around there's violence going on."

Pops was known throughout the neighborhood, and was considered a grandfather to all the neighborhood kids. While Ray was listening and taking in what Pops was saying to him, he just shook his head in disbelief. Even though Ray's life seemed to be getting better as the days went by, the city was continuing to go down because of senseless violence.

Noticing the hurt on Ray's face, Honey said, "Come on sweetie, get in the car, we're already running late for R.J.'s game. Don't worry; everything is going to be alright."

As Ray got in the car, and begun to drive off, he said to Honey, "We have to make a change babe, we can't continue to raise our son in this environment... It's time for a change."

As Ray and Honey arrived to the game, the parking lot was jammed packed, and you could feel the excitement in the air. High School basketball at Kingdom Prep wasn't like the normal high school basketball game, it was a way of life! The people in the community ate, slept, and breathed basketball at Kingdom Prep. As they got out of the car and begun to walk to the field house, they were amazed at how many people came out to the game. While walking into the gymnasium they noticed the tradition that filled the trophy cases. Championship after championship. That was the only standard that Coach Boyd understood at Kingdom Prep, and you could notice the players embraced that mentality. While R.J. was warming up, he was looking to see if he could spot his parents in the stands, but there were just too many people at the game. While R.J. went to lay the ball up, he heard his father say, "Do work R.J.!"

R.J. looked to his left, and there stood his mother and father with the biggest smiles on their faces. R.J. nodded his head at his father, and blew a kiss to his mother as he continued to warm up with his teammates.

As the game went on, Kingdom Prep dominated. It was evident that R.J. was part of a special group of guys who had one goal in mind, and that was to be the best basketball program in the nation. At the end of the game, Kingdom Prep won by 42 points, 101 to 59. R.J. finished the game with 22 points, 9 assists, 7 rebounds, and 6 steals. J-Mo and Reggie also played great with 23 and 17 points respectively.

Coach Boyd praised the boys after the game, and he spoke highly of his star freshman point guard R.J. Watkins. Every game after that one, brought about the same outcome night in and night out. Kingdom Prep was ranked the #1 team in the state, and the #3 team in the country, but they weren't satisfied with that ranking. They felt that they were the best. As the school year went on, and success continued to follow Kingdom Prep, as well as the new found popularity that R.J. was receiving, Coach Boyd continued to preach humility and hard work.

He never wanted his players to become wonderful in their minds, but to stay grounded and focused. Kingdom Prep went on to win the State Championship for a record 6 years in a row, and finished as the top ranked team in the country by USA Today High School basketball.

R.J. became a household name in the state, and across the country as everyone came to know of this slim 6 foot 3 inch point guard. He finished the season averaging 21.4 points, 8.7 assists, 6 rebounds, and 4 steals per game. His relationship with J-Mo had gotten better, and they became great friends. J-Mo also became R.J.'s mentor, which led to him becoming the #1 point guard in the country, and the #2 player in his class according to ESPN.com.

Every college in the nation was calling Coach Boyd about R.J., and he was only entering his sophomore season at Kingdom Prep. Coach Boyd never had a player of this caliber, who was as HIGHLY recruited as R.J. was. As for J-Mo, he accepted a scholarship from The University of Miami to play basketball for the Hurricanes.

The summer was about to be one of the most important summers of R.J.'s life, and without a doubt one of the busiest summers ever for the Watkins family.

CHAPTER 11

The school year was coming to an end, and the decision to choose which AAU team R.J. was going to play for was becoming very difficult for him. Every major shoe company had an AAU team from Nike, Adidas, Under Armor, and Reebok. Kingdom Prep was a Nike sponsored school, so R.J. was more than likely to lean towards the Nike AAU program All-Michigan Blue, which had almost every top player in the state on that team.

While R.J. sat on the front porch dribbling his basketball, Ray pulled into the drive way as he returned home from a long day at work. Ray got out of the car, he looked at R.J. and said, "Hey son, why do you look like you worked a twelve hour shift? What's on your mind?"

R.J. starred down at the porch, while dribbling the ball steadily with his left hand. He appeared to be in deep thought, still he replied, "Dad, I'm just trying to figure out this AAU stuff. This is a difficult decision to make. It seems like everyone is pulling me in a different direction, but at the same time I don't know who to trust, or if I will make the right decision."

Feeling the frustration from his son, Ray became irritated, because the one thing he didn't want to happen, was beginning to happen to R.J. Ray never wanted R.J. to become part of the recruiting circus, where major shoe corporations try to lure young athletes in via AAU programs.

Ray sat down next to R.J., and he said, "Listen son. Whatever you decide to do, do it for you and for you only! Your mother and I will support you in whatever decision you make, so don't feel pressured to do anything you don't want to do."

Looking up at his father, R.J. nodded his head and said, "You're right Dad, because no matter who I play with, its basketball. I want to play for the best and with the best players. So I know who I want to play for Dad... He laughs. "I'm going to play for All-Michigan Blue."

As Ray stood up to go in the house, he rubbed R.J. on the top of his head and said, "All-Michigan Blue it is Son. So get ready to work, because it's about to be a busy summer for you. I'll go in the house and call Coach Boyd to inform him of your decision, and don't worry yourself about this anymore son."

As Ray got to the door, R.J. said, "Hey Dad, thanks again for the advice." Smiling back at R.J., Ray said, "That's why I'm here son."

The school year was finally coming to an end. You could feel the excitement in the school because summer vacation was 20 minutes away. The students were all waiting for the final bell to ring. When it finally rang, it was as if a volcano had erupted. You could feel the vibration from the yells and screams released by the students.

As the students stormed the hallways, Mr. Whittier said over the P.A. system, "Congratulations to everyone on completing a great school year here at Kingdom Prep. I would also like to congratulate the graduating class, and acknowledge the continued success of our sports programs. Have a safe and blessed summer!"

While walking down the hallway with Reggie, R.J. asked him what his plans were for the summer. Reggie's father was a big time attorney, and his mother was one of the top Doctor's in the State of Michigan, as well as in the Midwest, so his parents were very well off financially. R.J. and Reggie become inseparable, though from two different worlds, they had the same goal, which was to play basketball at the highest level.

Reggie looked at R.J. and said, "Bro, we have like 5 trips we're going on this summer. I can never play AAU ball like I want to because my parents have things planned out a year in advance. They're really big on family trips and things like that."

R.J. had a look of amazement on his face, as he said to Reggie, "Did you just say five trips? Where is your family going? I have never taken five trips in my whole life."

Laughing at R.J.'s response, Reggie answered, "Bro, it gets pretty old and boring. My brother and I would love to just stay home for one summer, but we know that's not going to happen. We have to go on 2 cruises, Georgia for our family reunion, and then to Paris because my Mom wants to go there."

Shaking his head at Reggie, R.J. said, "Bro, you have the greatest life EVER! Man, my parents hate for me to go outside and play basketball in my neighborhood because it's so dangerous. I go to sleep to police sirens and gunshots every night, so count your blessings Reggie, and enjoy your summer."

Looking down at the floor as they walked down the hallway, Reggie replied, "Yea, I guess you're right R.J., sometimes it's easy to forget how fortunate I am, until I hear how others are living. I'm sorry bro."

Fanning his hand at Reggie, R.J. said, "Man you're cool, you didn't offend me at all, so there's no need for you to apologize. Just make sure you bring me something back from one of those trips."

R.J. and Reggie laughed as they walked down the hallway. Coach Boyd standing by his office door, saw them and said, "Hey fellas, are you two ready for the summer? Make sure you get a copy of our summer workout schedule. I expect the two of you to be here for workouts, and I don't want to hear about family vacations every other week Reggie."

Laughing at Coach Boyd, Reggie replies, "Coach, what do you want me to do? That's my parents, not me."

While shaking his head, Coach Boyd said to the boys, "You all enjoy your summer, and I will be seeing you two soon."

As R.J. and Reggie left out the school, they said their usual good-bye, "Manana," which meant tomorrow in Spanish. They gave each other a high five and a hug, then got in their respective rides and went their separate ways.

SUMMER VACATION...

The weather outside was scorching hot, and summer vacation was in full swing. As R.J. stood outside his home waiting for Coach Boyd to pick him up for workouts, Sammy stepped outside on his front porch with his friend Isaiah.

Sammy looked at R.J. then said sarcastically, "So if it's not the superstar himself, Mr. R.J. Watkins, long time no see my friend."

As R.J. looked at Sammy, he didn't say a word back to him, he just shook his head in disgust.

"Hey R.J., how you been man, I haven't seen you since middle school," said Isaiah.

R.J. looked at Isaiah and nodded his head, unsure if Isaiah was being sarcastic as well. He remained silent towards him also.

As Coach Boyd pulled up to the house to get R.J., Sammy yelled out while laughing, "You have a good day R.J., it was good seeing you for once!"

R.J. got inside the car, he put his hand in the air as if to say bye. Once he was in the car, Coach Boyd could tell that R.J. was aggravated, and something was troubling him, so he asked him, "What's going on R.J.? it seems like something is bothering you."

Without hesitation R.J. answered, "Coach, I just want to get out of this neighborhood. There's nothing but trouble over here and kids who want to start fights ALL the time!"

While listening to R.J. vent, Coach Boyd couldn't help but to think back to the days he lived in the same neighborhood on Asbury Park, just a few streets over from where R.J. was living.

"R.J., use your situation as motivation to get out of the hood, because complaining and being discouraged isn't going to make things better. Remember you're in a position to one day better the lives of your loved ones. So just stay focused and out of harm's way in the meantime."

Focusing in on what Coach Boyd had just said, R.J. nodded his head as he envisioned getting out of that neighborhood.

When R.J. and Coach Boyd arrived at the high school, the cheerleader's were practicing on one side of the gym floor. The cheerleading coach told Coach Boyd it was ok that they used the other half of the gym. Meanwhile, R.J. couldn't help but to notice one of the cheerleaders, Bianca Elyse. She was the prettiest girl in Kingdom Prep. All the boys wanted to be with her, but they were too intimidated by her beauty to approach her.

Noticing how hard R.J. was looking at Bianca, Coach Boyd jokingly said, "You can stop drooling all over yourself R.J."

While snapping out of his daze and laughing at the same time, R.J. said, "What are you talking about Coach?"

Coach Boyd laughed and shook his head. "Hurry up and get dressed, so we can start this work out."

Shortly after the workout began, the gymnasium became flooded with people; mostly those who just wanted an opportunity to watch R.J. Watkins workout in person. There were students, faculty members, and a number of media outlets from around the state present. While taking a water break, R.J. was amazed at the amount of attention he was getting, but at the same time he didn't like all the publicity.

As he stood at the free throw line, he looked at Coach Boyd and said, "Coach, why are all these people here? I'm just working out, it's not even that important."

Walking towards R.J. so nobody can read his lips, Coach Boyd said, "This comes with the territory R.J., you're the top player in the country, so everybody wants to be around success, always remember that."

Shaking his head like he always does, R.J. said, "Well, I guess Coach... I'm ready to finish up now."

They finished with the workout. An ESPN100 reporter was there to interview R.J. and Coach Boyd concerning the High School rankings, and R.J.'s plans for the summer AAU basketball circuit, as well as college interest. Not wanting R.J. to be overwhelmed by the media, Coach Boyd declined all interviews and told R.J. to go shower so he could get home.

While walking to the locker room, R.J. was met in the hallway by Bianca Elyse. Bianca's caramel skin, hazel eyes, and beautiful features were like none other. She stood at 5 feet 6 inches tall, and her slender medium athletic build drove the boys of Kingdom Prep crazy. As R.J. walked by, Bianca said to him, "How do you deal with all of that?"

Surprised that Bianca actually spoke to him, R.J. looked at her and said, "Honestly, I try to block it all out. By the way, my name is R.J. R.J. Watkins."

Laughing sheepishly at R.J., she replied, "I know who you are. Well, EVERYBODY knows who you are. My name is Bianca, Bianca Elyse."

While smiling at her as he wiped the sweat from his face, R.J. said, "I know who you are, well, EVERYBODY does."

They both laughed and continued to converse in the hallway, until Coach Boyd walked up and told R.J. to hurry up and get showered so he could get him back home. While walking away, R.J. stopped and turned back around, and asked Bianca if it would be okay if he called her sometime. With a huge flattered smile on her face, she happily told him yes.

CHAPTER 12

"R.J. get up son! You have to be at the airport in a couple of hours," yelled his Mother.

Total chaos was happening in the city. With many young people dying from senseless gun violence, R.J. was using basketball as an outlet and escape route. He was traveling to Las Vegas, Nevada to compete in the top Nike AAU basketball tournament in the country, the P.L.A.Y. Elite 25.

As R.J. woke up, he stretched and let out a loud scream that rang throughout the house. After sitting up in his bed, R.J. instantly got excited. He had been waiting for this tournament all summer. He competed in a total of 10 tournaments already, and scored at least 20 points in every game he played in. However, this was by far the biggest tournament of yet.

Ray walked by R.J.'s room. He stopped to look inside and said, "Let's get going son, we have to arrive at the airport early, and I hope you're well rested, because it's about to be a long day."

Looking up at his father, R.J. said, "Ok Dad, I'm getting up, and yea I got enough rest last night. I'm just ready to get to Vegas, it's going to be so much fun." Ray was happy to see R.J. living out his dream, and seeing his hard work pay off. When they went to church the previous Sunday, Bishop Theo laid hands on R.J and prayed for him, and it calmed the nervousness he had about flying in an airplane. Bishop

Theo prophesied to R.J. that he would be a globetrotter, and he would fly all over the world, and that his gift would make room for him, so because of that he will stand before great men.

That stuck in R.J.'s head, and he meditated on those words for two straight days. He could feel his confidence and boldness growing more and more, so he was more than ready for the tournament in Las Vegas.

R.J.'s summer was going great; his AAU team All-Michigan Blue had won every tournament they played in thus far. While R.J. tore up the AAU basketball circuit, his neighborhood was being torn up just as bad. Violence ran the streets of Detroit, even though Downtown was being rebuilt by a billionaire developer; the inner city was falling apart at a high rate. Vacant and burned down homes filled neighborhood streets. The murder rate was steadily on the rise, and very few if any of the young people had the outlet that R.J. had.

VEGAS...

Finally R.J. and his family made it to Las Vegas, and as R.J. sat in his hotel room his cell phone rung. R.J. answered his phone, and it was his friend Reggie calling from Macon, Georgia. His family was there for its family reunion that they attended every other summer.

"R.J., what's up man, how's your summer going? I'm in Georgia right now with my family, and its 97 degrees down here," Reggie said. R.J. busted out in laughter. "It's only 97 degrees there? Man, I'm in Vegas right now at this Nike tournament and we're afraid to go outside because its 114 degrees out there! We can't leave out of our rooms until the evening, unless we're playing a game."

"Are you serious!?" Reggie asked in disbelief. "It's really 114 degrees there? I would lose my mind in that type of heat!"

As they continued to speak on the phone, Reggie shared with R.J. what was next for him and his family on their summer tour as he called it. R.J. told him about all the tournaments he played in, and how well he had done. There was one thing that R.J. couldn't wait to tell Reggie.

"Bro, you wouldn't believe who I've been talking to all summer, and actually we really like each other."

Not knowing where to start, Reggie asked, "Who bro?" Don't make me try to guess, because I don't have ANY IDEA."

"You know her," R.J. said laughing. "Everybody in the school knows who she is. I'll give you a clue; she's the prettiest and most popular girl / cheerleader in the school, hint-hint."

After thinking for a moment Reggie yelled out, "BRO, not Bianca Elyse! R.J. Watkins, how did you pull that off? You are forever my hero bro."

As R.J. laughed with Reggie, he told him about how he and Bianca started talking, and that they talk almost every night on the phone. Reggie seemed to be more excited about R.J. and Bianca talking then R.J. was.

"Well bro, I'm happy for you, and keep me updated on everything! I'm about to go to dinner with my family now, so we'll talk when I get back home next week. Do work out there in Vegas bro, Manana." said Reggie, and they got off the phone.

The Las Vegas tournament had come to an end, and R.J. dominated the competition the entire week. He averaged an impressive 25 points, 9 assists, and 7 rebounds a game. He even hit the game winning shot that led them to victory over The Chicago Flames in a double overtime thriller. R.J. won the tournament MVP, and his team All-Michigan Blue won the Nike P.L.A.Y. Tournament Championship.

R.J. and his parents were finally heading to the airport to fly back home. As they sat and waited to board their plane, Ray looked out of the window of the airport, just to get a glance of the city one last time. Ray knew that it was back to reality in about six hours, and the thought of going back to work and beginning that grueling work schedule made him cringe. The trip to Vegas was great for Ray and his family. He and Honey got to watch R.J. play basketball against the best talent in the country, they spent time together as a family, and managed to spend some alone time with each other.

While in Vegas, Honey began coughing uncontrollably. They thought it was the humidity bothering her breathing, which caused her to cough. As they boarded the plane and took their seats, she started coughing again.

Ray looked at Honey and said, "Babe, are you ok? This has been going on for almost a week now, and it's not getting any better."

Wiping her mouth with some tissue she had, Honey said, "I'm ok sweetie, I believe it's just allergies, or maybe a respiratory infection from sitting in the air condition all day, then going out in the heat."

As R.J. listened to his parent's conversation, he had begun to get worried about his mother as well. He sat back and observed her.

Finally R.J. and his family made it back home to Detroit. As the plane landed at Metro Airport, the first person R.J. called was Bianca to let her know he made it back safely. Things were beginning to get real serious between the two of them. It was to the point where they couldn't go a day without talking to each other. Ray took notice of R.J.'s attachment to his cellphone, and the smiles that came with every phone conversation with Bianca. But as long as R.J. was focused, Ray didn't mind him having a girlfriend. Ray knew it was time for "the talk" between father and son, because R.J. was becoming of age and the puppy love he was experiencing was real.

While driving home from the airport, Ray looked over at Honey and noticed that she looked fatigued. Ray told her that he was going to take her to see their family doctor to make sure everything was ok. She didn't argue or disagree with Ray, she just said ok and sat quietly the rest of the ride home.

As they pulled up to their home, R.J noticed a group of guys standing on the curb in front of Sammy's house. As he got out of the car to go into the house, he noticed it was J.J. and his friends, and that they were all smoking weed. In disbelief, R.J. just shook his head and continued to take his bags in the house.

When R.J. came back outside to help his mother get her things in the house, J.J. yelled down the street, "Welcome home superstar, it's good to have you back amongst us little people."

The group of guys laughed, but Sammy didn't even look up because he was too embarrassed to do so. R.J. looked and didn't respond, walking in the house and closing the door behind him.

As R.J. got in the house, Ray said to him, "I heard what those guys said, so don't pay them any mind son. Those kinds of people will end up in one or two places, the grave or in prison. Remember that. You just make sure you stay focused!"

Looking up at his father, R.J. replied, "Yes Sir."

With the beginning of school a week away, and a great summer vacation coming to an end, R.J. found himself back in the gym working out with Coach Boyd. They sat down in the gym and spoke about R.J.'s summer, and what he enjoyed the most about it. R.J. didn't hesitate to say that Las Vegas was the most fun he ever had in his life. What made it even more memorable was his parents being there with him.

As R.J. and Coach Boyd sat in the gym talking, Reggie walked in the gym, and it seemed like forever since he had been in the gym.

Looking at Reggie as he walked up to them, Coach Boyd said, "Reggie, do you still play basketball young man? I literally haven't seen you ALL summer."

Looking at Coach Boyd with his mouth open, as if he couldn't find the words to speak, he finally said, "Coach, my parents had me and my brother on a world tour this summer, this is like FREEDOM for me to be in the gym, and to answer your question Coach, yes I still play basketball."

In typical R.J. fashion, he tried to break the ice by saying to Reggie, "Hey bro, did you bring me a shirt back from Paris?"

Reggie replied right back, "Did you bring me a shirt back from Las Vegas?"

They laughed, gave each other a high five and a hug, and then sat down on the bleachers to get dressed for their workout. Coach Boyd rolled the ball rack out onto the court, and told the guys to hustle up and get dressed. They only had the court for an hour before the cheerleading camp started.

Reggie couldn't help but to poke fun at R.J. by saying, "Coach, all we have to do is have R.J. tell Ms. Elyse to let us use half the gym."

Cutting his eyes at Reggie, R.J. gave him a sarcastic laugh while saying, "Very funny."

After their workout, Reggie was dead tired and for the first time he realized how out of shape he was. "Bro, I thought I was going to pass out on the court today," Reggie said.

Laughing at his buddy, R.J. said, "Man, you didn't look that bad. Then again, yes you did. Luckily you have time to get back in shape bro. As long as you're ready for the season, because right now, you look awful."

The boys laughed, then showered and got dressed to go home. Reggie's mom came and picked him up, and Coach Boyd took R.J. home as usual.

As they pulled up to R.J.'s home, R.J. realized his house keys weren't in his backpack, then he remembered they were sitting on his night stand in his room.

"Are you going to be okay R.J.," asked Coach Boyd. Frustrated that he forgot his keys, R.J. said to Coach Boyd, "Yes Sir, I'll just sit on the porch and wait for my parents to come home from the doctor's office."

Really hating that he had to sit and wait for his parents, R.J. didn't want to go with Coach Boyd either, so he sucked it up and waited there patiently.

While R.J. sat on the porch, Ray and Honey sat in the doctor's office waiting for the results from the tests performed on her earlier. Realizing that his wife was a bit nervous because of the uncertainty of what the results were going to be, Ray tried to lighten the mood by talking about different things to keep her mind off of it. After about a 45 minute wait, finally the doctor came into the room with the results to the test. Sitting down in the chair across from Ray and Honey, the doctor revealed the test results. It seemed like time slowed down as he spoke.

Honey was diagnosed with a rare form of respiratory cancer, and the doctor revealed that she was in the 3rd stage. In disbelief, and overcome with fear, Ray's eyes begun to fill up with tears. At a loss for words, he just looked at Honey. The doctor suggested that they start radiation and chemotherapy right away, to try to reverse the cancer while there was still a chance. Still in total shock and disbelief, Ray and Honey sat there as if they had just took a shotgun blast to the stomach, while at the same time trying to gather their thoughts. Ray began thinking about R.J. and how the news about his wife's diagnoses would affect him.

While taking a deep breath, Ray pulled himself together and said to Honey, "Babe, everything is going to be just fine. We will fight this thing together as a family."

Looking over at the doctor, Ray said to him, "Doc, what's next? Just say what it is you need us to do. You said something about chemotherapy and radiation how does that work?"

The doctor explained how the treatments would work, and how draining the whole process could be for Honey. The doctor then shared that some days would be better than others, and what the side effects would be for her. Honey just stayed quiet the whole time, with her eyes steadfast on the doctor as if she was absorbing all that he said.

Looking at Honey, Ray said, "Babe, are you ok with what the doctor is suggesting we do?"

Very calmly she replied, "Yes sweetie that's fine with me." Ray couldn't believe how in the matter of an hour his life took a 360 degree turn, for what seemed to be for the worse.

TRAGEDY STRIKES...

As R.J. sat on the porch, he began to get irritated because he had been waiting on his parents to get home for over an hour. While looking around, he noticed J.J. and his crew walking down the street, and they seemed to be up to no good. When J.J. got to the front of R.J.'s home, he stopped and stared him down as a form of intimidation. R.J. sat there looking at him, but he didn't say a word.

Looking to cause problems, J.J. said, "Hey superstar, do you have an eye problem or something? Because the way you're looking at me, is making me think you do.

R.J. continued to sit on the porch with a blank look on his face while ignoring J.J. Furious that he was being ignored; J.J. began to walk towards R.J.'s porch.

Without taking his eyes off of J.J., R.J. stood up and said, "Dude, don't come on my property starting problems. I don't even talk to you, so what's your issue?"

All in one motion, J.J. pulled out a gun and pointed it at R.J. and said, "You want to find out what my issue is superstar? You don't have much to say now do you?" The whole time R.J.'s eyes never went to the left or to the right, but he stayed focused on J.J.

R.J. was never scared, but more so upset and angry. With a sinister smile on his face, J.J. said, "You think you're so much better than everybody, because you go to that fancy school and you're some big time basketball star!"

As R.J. stood on the porch looking down the barrow of a 40 caliber pistol, Sammy came outside on his porch and noticed what was happening. Sammy's eyes got big, and he started running towards R.J.'s house yelling, "J.J. what are you doing?!"

Sammy ran across the grass towards J.J., and in one motion J.J. turned...

BANG! BANG!!

Not realizing what he had done out of pure panic, J.J. shot Sammy two times in the chest, dropping him to his knees. In disbelief, R.J. let out a loud scream as he watched Sammy crash to the ground face first. J.J. and his crew took off running up the street, while R.J. grabbed Sammy and tried to keep him conscious. The blood gushed out of his mouth as he tried to word "I'm sorry" to R.J. R.J. screamed for somebody to call an ambulance, but it was too late because Sammy had already died in his arms.

CHAPTER 13

The ride home from the doctor's office was a quiet one, Ray and Honey didn't say a word, but their minds seemed to race a hundred miles an hour with thoughts of the worse kind, and thoughts of a miracle happening. But the biggest thought was of R.J., and how he would take the news of his mother being diagnosed with cancer.

Finally after thirty minutes of silence, Honey said with a distressed and broken voice, "Ray, what are we going to tell R.J.? How are we going to tell this to our baby?

With tears building up in his eyes, Ray answered, "I don't know, I don't know."

When they finally reached their street, Ray and Honey noticed that it was flooded with people, and police cars blocked the street. Sudden fear came over them, when they noticed their home was taped off by the police.

Barely putting the car in park, Ray jumped out and ran towards his home with Honey close behind him. As they ran, fear built up, their adrenaline pumped with every stride they took. Ray and Honey were stopped short of their home by police officers.

Franticly Ray yelled, "That's our home!! We live there!! My son, is that him under that plastic?"

Ray was overwhelmed with fear, and Honey had become hysterical, with her face was covered with tears.

Suddenly, they heard a voice yell, "Mom-Dad!! I'm right here!" As they looked to their right, it was R.J. running towards them crying.

Ray and Honey cried as they hugged R.J. while asking him if he was ok, but at the same time wondering who was dead on their front yard.

Still crying, R.J. looked at his parents and said, "Its Sammy. He killed Sammy right in front of me. Sammy was trying to help me, and he turned and shot him." Unable to control his tears, R.J. just fell in his father's arms and wept and wailed for his friend.

Ray just held R.J., and he told him it was going to be alright, and then he stood R.J. up and looked him in his eyes to ask him who did that to Sammy.

Still crying, and angry at the same time, R.J. said, "It was J.J. Dad, he shot Sammy twice in the chest. He pulled the gun out on me, then Sammy came outside and seen what was going on. So he ran over to try to stop J.J., but he turned and shot him, then ran off."

In disbelief at what R.J. just told him, Ray just shook his head in disgust, then looked over at Honey and said, "Baby, we have to move. We have to. This is the final straw."

As Ray spoke, Sammy's mother, Mrs. Burns screamed and screamed to the top of her lungs, "My baby, my baby! These senseless murders have to stop!"

Honey hurriedly went over to give her emotional support, unable to imagine how much pain she was feeling. That night the neighbors had a vigil in honor of Sammy. Many in the neighborhood mourned because of his death. He was only 15 years old.

News had spread quickly about what happened in front of the Watkins home, mainly because R.J. was a well-known high school basketball star, and another young child was a victim of murder, gunned down viciously in the street. R.J.'s phone was being flooded with calls and text messages, with condolences and kind words from his friends.

Coach Boyd came by R.J.'s home to check on him, and to make sure he was coping with the death of his friend, as well as having witnessed the killing. Grief counselors came to their home, detectives were in and out, tons of reporters from local television stations and newspapers were frequently coming by or calling. Reggie and Bianca came by to see R.J., and it seemed like the only time he was himself was when they were around. They sat, laughed, and talked about the summer, but at times R.J. would get quiet and start talking to them about Sammy, and how he wished they could've met him because he was so funny. Bianca and Reggie just sat there and listened to R.J. vent, because they were there to support him, and help him get through this tough time in his life. They were by R.J.'s side every day, going to the mall, at the gym working out, or just sitting around the house playing cards or video games.

When R.J. went to the restroom, Ray walked in the family room and thanked Bianca and Reggie for being there for R.J. He told them how much it meant to him and his wife. The hardest thing for Ray was not telling R.J. about Honey being diagnosed with cancer on the same day his best friend was killed. It was difficult for them to hit him with that news at the time, knowing he was still dealing with Sammy's death.

As R.J. walked back in the family room, Ray looked at him and said, "How are you doing son? Are you hanging in there?"

With a slight smile on his face, R.J. said, "Yea dad, I'm doing ok... A lot better than I was a few days ago, I'm just ready for all this to be behind me." Nodding his head, Ray told him he understood what he meant, and that he needed to get some rest. Bianca and Reggie grabbed their things so they could leave.

R.J. gave Bianca a hug and kissed her on the cheek, then turned to Reggie and gave him a high five and said, "Manana bro."

After Bianca and Reggie left, R.J. went to his room and closed the door. As he lay on his bed, he closed his eyes and prayed. Thanking God for sparing his life the other day. R.J. cried until he fell asleep, hoping that the next day would

Chapter 14

With so much coming up within the next week, R.J. began to feel overwhelmed. Labor Day was on Monday, school was the following day, and Sammy's funeral was being held on Friday. Because R.J. had seen Sammy get killed, the prosecutor requested he come to trial as a key witness to testify against J.J. As result of the tragedy, R.J.'s parents started looking for a new home, even if it meant staying in an apartment for a while, they just wanted to get out of the city.

Honey sat in the kitchen on her laptop searching the Internet endlessly for a home. Ray was at the counter preparing the meat for the holiday, while R.J. and his friends sat in the family room playing video games. There was a knock at the door. Honey went to open it. To her surprise it was Mrs. Burns, Sammy's mother. She asked if R.J. was home because she needed to speak to him. Honey called for him to come up front, and when he saw Mrs. Burns standing in the living room, his heart sunk within him.

Looking at her, R.J. could see the restlessness and pain in her eyes, but somehow she was able to find strength in the midst of what had happened to Sammy.

"R.J., I came down here to ask you, if you'll do me the honor of being one of Sammy's pallbearers," said Mrs. Burns.

As R.J. stood there looking at her, grief overtook him and the tears begun to flow down his face, however, he found enough strength to tell her yes. Mrs. Burns hugged R.J. to console him, and then told him that everything was going to be alright. She reassured him of how much Sammy loved and looked up to him.

R.J. wiped the tears from his face and said to Mrs. Burns, "Thank you for choosing me to be a pallbearer. I will never forget Sammy as long as I live. He was the brother that I never had, and I'm going to miss him like crazy."

Mrs. Burns thanked Honey for letting her speak to R.J., and as she turned to leave out, she said to them, "You all have a good evening, and God bless you all."

R.J. just sat on the living room couch in total disbelief. He still couldn't believe that Sammy was dead, and that he would never see him again. Looking up at his mother, R.J. said, "Mom, I don't know if I'll be able to participate at the funeral, it's going to be hard seeing Sammy lying there like that."

As she rubbed the top of his head, she told him to just think of all the fun times they had together, and to relive them in his mind daily, because that's how he'll be able to keep Sammy's spirit alive.

R.J. listened to what his mother said, and then went back into the family room where Bianca and Reggie were. As R.J. walked into the family room, Bianca could tell he had been crying, so she asked him was everything okay. R.J. explained to them that Sammy's mother had come over and asked him to be a pallbearer, and how just the thought of everything overwhelmed him. "Everything just seems so unreal to me, I guess it REALLY hasn't hit me yet," said R.J.

THE TOUGHEST DAY EVER...

The holiday had come and gone, R.J.'s second year of high school had started, and the most dreadful day of his life had quickly approached. Dressed in a black suite, a white shirt and black tie, R.J. sat on his bed wondering what the day was going to bring. Trying to envision the funeral and how everything was going to play out, not knowing how he was going to feel or react to seeing Sammy lying in a coffin.

Ray came and stuck his head in R.J.'s room to make sure he was doing ok, and to let him know it was time to leave for the funeral. With his palms sweating and a ton of nervous energy coming over him, R.J. put his head down and told his father he'd be right out.

While trying to gather his thoughts, R.J. took a few deep breaths and said to himself, "Let's get this over with R.J."

As he got in the car, Ray looked back at him and asked, "Are you doing okay son? No need to worry, everything is going to be alright."

Without responding to his father, R.J. just nodded his head as if to say okay. Yet, Ray knew it was hard for R.J. to handle what had happened to Sammy, and that he needed all the support he could get.

When they pulled up to the church where the funeral was being held, R.J. was met by his girlfriend Bianca.

As he greeted her with a hug, he took a deep breath and said, "Okay, it's time to get this over with… Ready or not here we go."

As they walked into the sanctuary it was jammed packed with family, old classmates, neighbors, and at least 50 gang members were lined up around the walls from a gang Sammy was supposedly in, they all came out to pay their respects to him. While walking down the aisle towards the casket, the song "Yesterday" by Mary-Mary played in the background. Ray walked on R.J.'s left side while Bianca was on his right.

With each step R.J. could feel knots forming in his stomach. When he got to the casket he felt chills, and then sudden warmth, and finally anxiety over took him and he burst into tears crying uncontrollably. Ray held R.J. as he comforted him and told him it was ok, and Bianca took R.J. by the hand and walked him to his seat.

As the funeral service went on, there were many laughs and many tears shed as they reflected on Sammy's life. A young boy was gone too soon, and what he could have been will always be unknown. Even though Sammy made some bad choices in his short life, his last decision to stand up for a friend was what R.J. would always remember.

When Ray and R.J. returned home from the funeral, Honey was lying on the bed sleep. Ray kneeled by the side of the bed and held her hand, then looked at her. Thoughts ran through his head about possibly losing his wife. Tears instantly fell from his eyes as he laid his head on her shoulder.

R.J. walked by his parent's bedroom. He noticed his father kneeling on the side of the bed. R.J. knew something was wrong with his mother, but he didn't know the seriousness of her illness. "Dad, is everything ok? What's wrong with Mom, and why are you crying?" While R.J. continued to spit out questions to his father, his mother opened her eyes. R.J. could see the weakness in her eyes and hear it in her voice as she said quietly, "Come over here and sit next to me son, your father and I have something we need to tell you."

Not knowing what to expect, R.J. went and sat next to his mother on the edge of the bed. With her eyes weakened, and feeling fatigued from the chemotherapy session earlier in the day, Honey said to him, "Son, the doctor gave me some bad news two weeks ago concerning my health. I have cancer in my lungs, but hopefully with these chemo treatments I'll be fine."

Taken back by what his mother just told him, R.J. sat up on the edge of the bed and shook his head in disbelief. Just hours ago R.J. buried his best friend since the age of five, and now his mother has told him she was terminally ill with cancer. To hear the word cancer is like hearing 'your days are numbered,' because cancer is what took R.J.'s grandfather's life five years ago.

Putting his hand on R.J.'s back, Ray said, "Son, we wanted to wait and tell you because of what happened to Sammy. Everything is going to be just fine; your mother is going to be okay. We will fight this thing together as a family."

Honey looked at R.J, and she hated to see him deal with so much hurt at a young age. It was unfair for him to have to deal with so much, but her job was to help him be strong, even in her weakness.

"R.J., don't worry about me son. You're strong, and you will get through this because God will not put more on us then we can bear. Whatever the outcome may be, know that I love you son, and you have made me proud."

With tears rolling down his face, R.J. kissed his mother on the cheek, and told her that he loved her.

"Okay Son, we need to let your mother rest so she can get her strength back up," Ray said with tears in his eyes.

R.J. tucked his mother in with her comforter, and then kissed her on the cheek again before leaving the room.

As R.J. went to his room, he fell back on his bed and looked at the ceiling. His mind raced nonstop with thoughts of Sammy lying in that casket, and of his mother possibly dying from cancer. R.J. was slowly falling into a state of depression, and was unsure how to deal with all of the emotions that were building up. He turned to the person that was always there for him, and knew how to help him channel his emotions in the right direction, and that was Coach Boyd.

R.J. picked up his cell phone and called Coach Boyd, and asked if he could pick him up so they could work out. Through all the chaos that was going on in R.J.'s life, the basketball court was the only place he could find peace. It was his personal sanctuary and temporary stress reliever.

Coach Boyd told R.J., if it was okay with his parents he'll be there to pick him up in thirty minutes. R.J. asked his father if it was okay to go to the gym with Coach Boyd, and Ray told him it was fine. Ray felt R.J. needed to get out of the house and do something positive, and working out with Coach Boyd was perfect.

While R.J. was in his room getting ready to go with Coach Boyd, Ray walked in to make sure R.J. was okay. "Hey son, just making sure you're alright. I know this is a lot on you, but I want you to know that we're in this together, okay?"

With a smile on his face, as he shook his head, R.J. said, "I'm good Dad, and yea it is a lot, but like you and Mom always taught me, I have to learn to adapt to change, and deal with life happening. I'll be alright."

Coach Boyd knocked on the front door, and Ray greeted him as he came in. Ray asked Coach Boyd to have a seat at the kitchen table, and as they sat down he informed Coach Boyd about what was going on with his wife. While he took in the news, Coach Boyd's heart felt like it fell into his stomach.

He kept telling Ray, "I'm sorry."

Ray told him it was ok, and then thanked him for picking up R.J. to get him out of the house.

Coach Boyd understood why it meant so much to get R.J. out of the house, and then said, "I'm here if you need me Mr. Watkins."

CHAPTER 15

The school year was in full swing, and so much had changed in R.J.'s life within the past few months. He no longer had his best friend down the street, and his mother was battling cancer. The one thing that was going well in his life besides basketball was his relationship with Bianca. They had been steady for almost 3 months, and she was there for R.J. through all the turmoil in his life. They did everything together, from going to football games, eating lunch, to studying. Bianca's father was the Pastor at the church Reggie and his family attended out in the suburbs, but she never spoke about her parents.

Her father wasn't home much because he was always busy doing church work, and her relationship with her siblings was odd and very distant. Her mother was quiet and kept to herself a lot, rarely speaking to Bianca. Bianca always admired R.J.'s relationship with his parents, so she spent a lot of time with them as a family, and really became close to R.J.'s mother.

As Bianca and R.J. walked down the hallway at school, she reminded him that his father was going to be late picking him up from school. R.J. totally forgot about his mother's chemotherapy treatment, and he knew that was the reason his father was going to be late.

"I really wanted to be there with my mom today. I hate to see her go through this Bianca, because I know how she used to be. Now she's always tired and weak," said R.J. with depression in his voice.

While grabbing R.J.'s hand, Bianca said, "I understand what you're saying, and I feel your pain babe. Your mother is such a strong lady. I believe she's going to pull through this."

R.J. smiled. He couldn't help but to feel happy to have her in his life, "Thanks B. I appreciate you being here for me. I really do."

As R.J. went to kiss Bianca, Reggie ran up and said, "Hey-hey, you two cut it out! No smooching in the hallway, especially you Preacher's daughter."

R.J. laughed, "What do you want Reginald Curtis?"

Reggie shook his head. "I'm going to the gym to get some shots up. Do you want to come with me?"

Honestly, R.J. really didn't feel like working out, but Bianca encouraged him to do so while he waited for his father. As R.J. kissed Bianca on the cheek, he told her he would call her later, then turned to Reggie and said, "Come on bro, let's get a quick workout in before my dad gets here, Lord knows I need a stress reliever."

As R.J. and Reggie walked down the hall to the gym, they were met by Coach Boyd. "R.J., you're just the person I was looking for," Coach said to him. "What time is your ride coming to get you?"

Looking puzzled, R.J. told Coach Boyd that his father was going to pick him up late, because his mother had to take her chemo treatment. Coach Boyd told R.J. he would call his father to ask if he could bring him home, because there were college coaches at the school to see him workout.

"Coach, I just wanted to get some shots up. Do we have to do an "all-out" workout?" asked R.J. Looking at R.J. with a blank look on his face, Coach Boyd said, "Well, I will tell Duke, Kentucky, North Carolina, UConn, Michigan, Michigan State, and Arizona you don't feel like working out today."

R.J. looked at Reggie in amazement because of the schools Coach Boyd had just mentioned. "Coach, Reggie and I will be ready in 5 minutes."

Coach Boyd laughed. "That's what I thought. You two hustle up and get dressed," he said as he walked away.

Just as the workout came to an end, Ray walked into the gym. He couldn't believe the amount of people that were there watching the boys workout. While Ray stood up against the wall, he noticed the coaches that were in the gym, and when they realized who he was, they bombarded him with handshakes, cards, and conversation. Ray couldn't help but to think back to when R.J. was a little boy, and how far he had come in what seemed to be such a short time.

As R.J. was leaving the court, he looked over at his father with a smile and nodded his head. R.J. wooed the coaches during his workout, and more importantly UConn was so impressed by Reggie, that they offered him a scholarship.

"Hey Mr. Watkins," said Coach Boyd as he walked up to Ray. "How's everything going? I told R.J. I would call you to let you know that I would bring him home."

"Its fine Coach, I wanted to come up. Besides I figured he would be in the gym working out anyway. I just never thought all these coaches and people would be in here watching them workout."

Coach Boyd told Ray that it was unexpected, and coaches had one more week to come out and see players. While they were yet talking, R.J. and Reggie came out of the locker room, and Reggie was smiling from ear to ear because of the scholarship offer he just received.

"Why are you cheesing so hard Reggie," asked Ray. Still smiling from ear to ear, Reggie said to Ray, "Mr. Watkins, if you just received an offer from UConn, wouldn't you be cheesing too?" Ray laughed at Reggie and said, "Well, I guess you do have a reason to smile… Congratulations big fella!"

As they finished speaking with the coaches, Ray told R.J. they had to hurry up and leave, so they could get home to check on his mother. Honey wasn't feeling well after her chemotherapy treatment, so Ray wanted to make sure she was doing ok.

While they were walking to the door, Ray said to Coach Boyd, "I appreciate all you do Coach, thanks again." Coach Boyd gave him a thumbs up and nodded his head.

During the ride home Ray and R.J. talked about the colleges that were at the school and which school R.J. liked the most. Without hesitation, R.J. said, "Duke!"

Ray and Honey were HUGE Michigan fans. Ray said with a shocked voice, "Really? Duke? Coach K?"

Laughing at his father, R.J. said, "I'm just kidding dad, I really like Michigan, Kentucky, and Arizona in that order. Coach K is a great coach, but I don't see myself playing there."

Ray wiped his forehead, as if he was wiping away sweat. "Whew, you had me going for a minute son, I never expected you to say that," he said laughing. "But I would have supported your decision, now your Mother, I'm not too sure."

"Speaking of Mom, how is she doing Dad? I'm really worried about her. Have you thought about taking her to Bishop Theo, so he can pray for her? He said at the welcoming assembly at school, that God healed him from cancer."

Taking in everything R.J. said, Ray just nodded his head and said, "Son, your Mother has her good days, and she has her bad days. Today was a bad day for her, because the chemo treatments make her sick sometimes. As for Bishop Theo, I thought about that a few times, but I never knew he had cancer before. Son, maybe we'll do that.

Well, let's say this; we will do that this Sunday. In the meantime, we have to keep your Mother's spirits up."

R.J. didn't know how to feel, he had faith and believed God could heal his mother, but it was easier said than done, especially when staring the situation in the face. With everything seeming to go so well with basketball, Bianca, and school, the thought of losing his mother overshadowed all of that. Basketball didn't seem as important anymore, and the fight against depression started to wear on R.J. like a coat.

THE TOUCH...

The weekend had come, and Ray had already spoken to Honey about going to church so Bishop Theo could pray for her. She thought it was a good idea, and agreed to go even though she was feeling weak in her body. When they made it to church, it was packed as usual, and Bishop Theo was just getting up to preach. The sermon he preached was powerful, he spoke about the woman who had the issue of blood for 12 years, and it seemed like that particular word was for Honey and right on time. When Bishop Theo finished preaching, he asked if there was anyone that wanted prayer. Feeling inspired and full of faith, Honey jumped up without hesitation.

"Babe, let me help you," said Ray, but Honey was focused on getting to the altar.

Honey believed God for her healing, so she acted on it, and went to get prayer from Bishop Theo. As Ray walked with her to the altar for prayer, he held her by the hand and she walked close by his side. Not knowing what to expect, Bishop Theo asked Honey to raise her hands. As he laid his hands on her head, she felt warmth go through her body, and then tears began to flow down her face uncontrollably.

After Bishop Theo prayed for her, he hugged her and said, "Man can give a diagnosis, but it's God that gives the prognosis. All is well."

Trying to hold back his tears, Ray turned to Honey and hugged her, and then slowly walked her back to their seats.

During the ride home from church, Honey couldn't stop crying no matter how hard she tried. With a look of concern on his face, R.J. said, "Mom, are you okay?"

Looking at R.J. through the rearview mirror, Ray said, "She's okay son, your Mother is just grateful and thankful that we serve a great God."

Not understanding what his father meant, R.J. just shook his head and said, "Okay dad."

Honey slightly turned around to look at him and said, "Son, I realized two things at church today. The first thing is that God is able to heal me. Second, if he doesn't heal me, he's still able, and he is still God. R.J., whatever state you find yourself in during this lifetime son, just remain content and always trust God."

Looking his mother in her eyes, R.J. nodded his head and said, "Yes Ma'am."

Finally home, Ray sat at the kitchen table to finish up some reports for work. Honey was in their bedroom asleep, and R.J. was in the family room watching the Detroit Pistons play the L.A. Lakers in the 2004 NBA Finals on NBA television.

As R.J. watched the game he received a text from Bianca, it seemed like she always knew when to say the right things, at the right time. R.J. was feeling down because of his mother's condition, and he knew the reality of her possibly dying was real. Bianca's text made R.J. smile, she simply texted him, "Smile, and know that I love you!!"

With the high school basketball season a month away, R.J. envisioned himself playing for an NBA championship as he watched the game. R.J. vaguely remembered being on the court for the Piston's championship win, Ray was friends with former Detroit Piston Lindsey Hunter, and R.J. was 6 years old when they won the championship.

While R.J. was watching the game, Ray walked in the room and saw what was on the television. Ray said with a huge smile on his face, "Wow! That brings back SO many memories son. That was a special team they had, and I never seen your Uncle Lin so happy. I need to call him to see how he's doing; I haven't spoken to him in a while."

With his eyes steadied on the television, but still hearing what his father had said, R.J. said, "Dad, I'm worried about Mom. I pray she pulls through, because I can't see myself in the NBA without her there." As Ray sat down next to R.J., he took a deep breath and said, "Son, I can't imagine her NOT being here at all." They both just sat quietly on the couch in deep thought.

CHAPTER 16

Another school year had come and gone, and a busy summer for R.J. was coming to an end. So the time for him to make a decision about what college he would be attending, was coming up soon. While people waited in anticipation to hear where R.J. would go, choosing a college was the furthest thing from his mind. He spent almost every free moment he had next to his mother.

Honey had started to regain her strength, and the cancer seemed to have gone into remission, but she became very sick again. It devastated R.J., so, he wasn't thinking about basketball at all.

Coach Boyd had become very concerned about R.J., because he had missed 3 out of 5 mandatory summer workouts the team had. It was unlike R.J. to miss workouts, because he used them as an outlet or what he called a "stress reliever."

He called R.J. to check on him, to make sure he was doing okay, but he wasn't able to reach him, instead he got the voicemail.

"R.J., this is Coach Boyd checking in with you. Give me a call when you get a chance Big Fella. Okay, I'll talk to you soon."

Just as Coach Boyd hung up the phone, R.J. walked into his office. Surprised to see R.J. walking in, Coach Boyd said, "Hey R.J., I just called you. How's it going? I was beginning to worry about you, because I haven't seen nor heard from you in a week."

As R.J. sat down in a chair across from Coach Boyd, he said, "Coach, I apologize for missing workouts and not calling, but this is really a tough time for me and my family. I've just needed some time to sort things out."

Coach Boyd could see the stress and worry in his eyes. His heart went out to him. "I understand R.J., I really do. Take as much time as you need to sort things out. Now I have one question. When you say "sort things out," what does that really mean?"

After taking a deep breath R.J. shrugged his shoulders at the same time, R.J. looked at Coach Boyd and said, "Coach, basketball isn't that important to me right now, I mean, my mother is fighting for her life. She is a major part of my success and my drive. It's just tough for me now coach."

Nodding his head as if to say okay, Coach Boyd said, "I support you R.J., just take your mind off of basketball for now, and make sure you focus on family. How did you get up here? Do you need a ride home? R.J. told him he didn't need a ride home, because Bianca was outside waiting on him.

As R.J. walked out of the office, Coach Boyd said, "R.J., you hang in there, and if you need anything don't hesitate to call me. We're family. Love you Big Fella."

Smiling at Coach Boyd, R.J. said, "I love you too Coach." As R.J. got in the car with Bianca, he took a deep breath and reclined his seat all the way back. Bianca looked at him and asked, "How did it go? Is everything ok?" Not knowing how to answer her question, R.J. just shrugged his shoulders and said, "I don't know."

For the first time ever, R.J. felt a separation between him and basketball. The one thing that seemed to give him life, all of a sudden felt so distant.

With a look of concern on her face, Bianca said, "R.J. Watkins, you didn't quit the basketball team did you?"

Shaking his head, R.J. replied, "No B, I would never do that. I just need some time to sort things out and spend time with my Mom."

Feeling relieved, Bianca said, "Ok, I understand. You've worked too hard to quit, and I want to see you succeed, as well as your Mom and Dad. Everything is going to be ok babe, just know that."

He said nothing; R.J. just nodded his head as if to say okay.

Bianca hated to watch R.J. go through another difficult time. It had been two years since Sammy died, and now he had to deal with his mother battling cancer.

As they were riding in the car, R.J. got a text message from Reggie, asking if he and Bianca wanted to come over and hang out for a few hours. R.J. was kind of hesitant because he wanted to get back home, but he asked Bianca if she wanted to go. Bianca told him it was okay with her, as long as he cheered up a little.

"Babe, I want you to have fun and enjoy yourself, you know, laugh a little more. You can't pray and worry R.J.

R.J. looked at Bianca and said, "You're right B. I can't pray and worry, actually I never thought about it like that. Wow. Thanks Bianca, I know I tell you this all the time, but I TRULY mean it, you are such a blessing to my life."

Blushing, she replied, "That's because I love you R.J. Watkins, and I'll always be here for you."

As the day came to an end, Bianca dropped R.J. off at home. R.J. felt refreshed from the time he spent with his friends. They laughed, played video games, and talked about college. For the first time in a long time, he had no worries and felt normal. When R.J. walked in the house, he was surprised to find his mother watching television in the family room. R.J. took a seat next to her. "Hey Mom, what are you watching? I didn't expect to find you in here."

While lying back on the couch, Honey said, "Son, I got tired of lying in the bed all day, and I feel a lot better today than I've felt in a long time; so I figured I'd watch a little TV."

R.J. was happy to hear his mother was feeling better. He told her about his day, as well as the meeting he had with Coach Boyd.

As they were talking, Ray walked in the family room and sat down on the floor in front of the couch. "Hey you two, what did I miss?"

Looking over at R.J., Honey said, "Go ahead son, tell your father about the meeting you had with Coach Boyd earlier today."

Feeling embarrassed, R.J. exhaled while looking down at the floor, and then explained to his father what he and Coach Boyd met about earlier that day.

Frustrated with R.J., but at the same time he understood how he felt, Ray said, "Son, your mother and I always taught you that life is about making adjustments, and that you have to make them when adversity comes. So walking away from your responsibilities isn't making the right adjustments."

Gently looking over at R.J., Honey said to him, "Sweetie, don't miss anymore workouts or practices. I'm going to be alright son, so don't worry about me! You've worked too hard to be in the position you're in, and the best is yet to come, so continue to make us proud."

With tears welling up in his eyes, R.J. hugged his parents and apologized, but Ray told him there was no need to apologize. They understood the emotional decision he made.

From that day forward, R.J. pursued basketball like never before. He dedicated his junior season to his Mother, which resulted in another undefeated season, #1 Ranking, and 3rd consecutive State Championship in as many years there. R.J. had another stellar year by averaging 26 points, 8 assists, and 6 rebounds. He finished his junior season as a first team All-State selection, and he received Conference Player of the Year Award for the second straight season.

That following summer went great for R.J. He played for the USA's 17 and under World Championship team over in Rio De Janeiro, Brazil, where they competed against the best talent in the world. He led the team in assists and steals, while being third in scoring. R.J. watched his mother beat cancer, and got to see his buddy Reggie off to college at UConn. He and Bianca's relationship was strong, and the excitement of being a senior in high school was evident.

THE DECISION...

The time had finally come for R.J. to make a decision concerning which college he would attend in the fall. His three choices were the: University of Michigan, University of Arizona, and the University of Kentucky. As R.J. entered the field house where he would make his announcement, the students and faculty gave him a standing ovation as they screamed and cheered his name. Nervous, R.J. took a seat at the table with his parents with Coach Boyd joining him. R.J. thanked everyone at Kingdom Prep, his parents, Coach Boyd, and Bishop Theo for supporting him throughout his career.

With three hats sitting on the table, each hat represented one of three colleges. R.J. spoke highly of each school, but there could only be one choice. Taking a deep breath, R.J. said without hesitation, "Next year I will be attending The University of Michigan!"

The Fieldhouse erupted in cheers. Honey cried tears of joy; Ray clapped his hands uncontrollably, while Coach Boyd patted R.J. on the back and told him he was proud of him. The University of Michigan had landed the #1 point guard in the country, and the #3 player overall.

As R.J. looked in the crowd to find Bianca, he had seen that she was crying and clapping. When R.J. caught eye contact with her, he winked his eye, blew a kiss, and yelled, "GO BLUE!"

Happy that the weight of choosing a school was finally off his back, R.J. could now focus on finishing out his senior year with no extra stress. As he walked to his locker, he received a text message from Reggie congratulating him on signing with the University of Michigan. Reggie was already in college, so R.J. had to get used to life without his friend again like in the past. Nevertheless, R.J. persevered through his senior season by winning the Mr. Basketball Award as the top player in Michigan, and being named to the McDonald's All-American team. R.J. received numerous awards, so many, they didn't have enough room to store them at home. Ray and Honey were extremely proud of R.J., and what he had accomplished, therefore everything he had done in life brought honor to them. The next step was college.

THE UNEXPECTED...

As R.J. moved into the dorms at U of M, Bianca was right there by his side. She had received a cheerleading scholarship from the University of Michigan, and R.J. was excited to have her there with him for the next 4 years. R.J. had received a copy of their basketball schedule, and he saw where they would be playing UConn in Puerto Rico during a basketball tournament.

He quickly called Reggie and told him to get ready to lose when they play each other in Puerto Rico. They shared some laughs, and bragged on the schools they were at, and as they got off the phone, they told each other how much they missed one another, and then ended with their usual "Manana."

After realizing it was his mother's birthday, R.J. told Bianca he wanted to go home to surprise her. Agreeing that it was a good idea, they planned out how they were going to surprise her, by deciding to pop up at the house with a birthday cake and ice cream. R.J. thought it would be a good idea to tell his father about the surprise, but then figured it would be cool, if his father didn't know either.

As they drove home R.J. thought it would be good to ride through his old neighborhood, because he hadn't been over there in almost two years. When he rode down the street, he couldn't believe how different the neighborhood was, and how much of a ghost town it had become. While riding through the neighborhood, an eerie feeling came over R.J. which he didn't like.

R.J. had gotten hungry, and asked Bianca to stop at the Coney Island restaurant so he could grab something quick to eat. As R.J. walked in the restaurant, everyone knew who he was, and the people came up to him and shook his hand, gave him encouraging words, and the owner let R.J. get his food for free.

While thanking everyone and saying his good byes, R.J. walked out of the door and couldn't believe who he had walked into…it was J.J. Out of jail early after his lawyer convinced a jury that he acted in self-defense, R.J. stood face to face with the guy who killed his best friend four years ago. R.J. froze up.

"R.J. Watkins…, the last time I seen you was in court, and because of you I spent four years in prison," said J.J.

Not knowing what to do, R.J. tried to walk by J.J. but he and his friends blocked him in and wouldn't let him pass.

"Look J.J., I don't want any problems, so just let me get in the car and leave," R.J. said.

While sitting in the car, Bianca could tell something was wrong, so she rolled down the window to make sure everything was ok… "R.J. is everything alright babe?"

Trying to stay calm, R.J. told Bianca that everything was fine, and to roll the window back up. Hesitating for a moment, Bianca rolled the window up, and as she did so, she could see R.J. forcefully trying to get pass J.J. and his friends. As Bianca was getting out of the car, she heard gun shots fired.

Bang! Bang! Bang!

As the crowd dispersed, R.J. lay in front of the restaurant door bleeding from his chest, his University of Michigan shirt was becoming immersed with blood.

Feeling his life slipping away, R.J.'s mind raced back in time as if it was replaying his life over to him. Thoughts of Sammy, his parents, Coach Boyd, Bishop Theo, his success... It all flashed before his eyes.

Frantic and shaking, Bianca screamed for help as she tried to talk to R.J. to keep him conscious.

"Baby, keep your eyes open. R.J. hold on baby, help is coming!" As R.J. lay there, he held Bianca's hand as he gasped for breath and his eyes slowly faded to black.

"R.J.! R.J.!" yelled Bianca, but he was gone.

R.J. Watkins was pronounced dead at the scene.

There are very few that make it out of the hood, and R.J. was one that defied the odds, that soared high, but had his dream and life snatched from him, right at the pinnacle of greatness. The very evil his parents successfully protected him from as a child, was the very thing he went back to…the violence of the hood. Ironically that past Sunday, Bishop Theo preached a sermon entitled, "Don't look back." Even as God sent angels into Sodom and Gomorrah to rescue Lot and his family, He sent basketball to rescue R.J. Watkins. However, just like Lot's wife, R.J. looked back. *"Remember Lot's wife!" Luke 17:32.*

What could've been the legend of R.J. Watkins will never be known. Ray and Honey watched their son overcome adversity, live through pain, and triumph over defeat. Only in the end, they seen their pride and joy taken away too soon, and it was devastating. The Life of The Black

Athlete is one of perseverance and endurance. However, in the end, "We're all just a kid from somewhere... trying to make it..."

...The End

CPSIA information can be obtained
at www.ICGtesting.com
Printed in the USA
BVOW07s1657050317
477585BV00018B/91/P

9 780989 430722